"Funny, we're all still talking around here as if it were the middle of January, not March and close to Spring Festival. I keep thinking it's as if time had stopped, or something."

He went to the window in the upper part of the cellar door and looked out.... A few new flakes were falling lazily. "I wonder if time *has* stopped," Jed said softly, watching them drift down. "I wonder if that could be what's gone wrong..."

"Are you serious?" asked Melissa. She wondered briefly if he might be joking, but something in his face when he turned back told her he wasn't.

"An evocatively drawn setting provides a perfect background as Garden subtly and smoothly styles her plot, straddling the fantasy-realism line in a convincing yet titillating way...[an] intriguing story."—(starred review) *Booklist*

"This book—with its cipher, folklore touches and attractive cover—is likely to satisfy all..."
—*School Library Journal*

FOURS CROSSING

by
NANCY GARDEN

Vagabond Books

SCHOLASTIC BOOK SERVICES
New York Toronto London Auckland Sydney Tokyo

ISBN 0-590-32287-7

Copyright © 1981 by Nancy Garden. All rights reserved. This edition published by Scholastic Book Services, a division of Scholastic Inc., 50 West 44th St., New York, N.Y. 10036, by arrangement with Farrar, Straus & Giroux, Inc.

12 11 10 9 8 7 6 5 4 3 2 1   3   2 3 4 5 6 7/8

To Lorelle, David, and Lise Paul,
with love

When Melissa Dunn first saw the little village of Fours Crossing, New Hampshire, from the train window, most of it was hidden behind clouds of snow that swirled from a dim and gloomy sky. "Don't dwell on sad things, Melissa," her mother had always told her. But it was hard not to on this dreary late afternoon at the end of a winter when her Boston home had seemed as cold as Maine and grayer, most days, than in the wettest, darkest spring.

The trouble had started in late fall, when Melissa's mother suddenly lost weight and then her normal, bustling cheerfulness. Not long after that, Melissa began to hear her moaning at night with pain. When Mum went into the hospital on the first snowy day in November, Melissa felt a knot of fear lodge inside her, pulling tighter as she realized the doctors had stopped predicting when her mother might get well.

Then one afternoon in mid-February her mother died. Melissa's father was so numb with grief that it fell to Melissa to soothe the relatives and answer the letters, cook the meals and clean the house. "So capable for someone who's just turned thirteen," an aunt said of her admiringly — but the praise didn't seem important. Nothing did. Every time Melissa tried to talk with her father about her mother, his bewildered eyes filled with tears, forcing her to hold back her own to comfort him. And now Melissa, who had always been such a talker that at school it had been a class joke, found she could no longer say much at all to anyone, at least not about anything that mattered.

Melissa looked out the window as the train, a twice-a-week ski special, crept onto a narrow bridge that spanned a frozen river. She wondered if it was the river Daddy had told her marked Fours Crossing's town line. If so, her long trip was over, for Fours Crossing was where she was going to stay with her grandmother while her father made one last trip as a traveling fund raiser before looking for a settled-down job in Boston. He'd promised Melissa that as soon as he finished this last assignment he'd resign from the firm that for years had sent him to faraway towns to raise money for charities — or, as with this trip, from state to state looking for new clients. "All over the country," Melissa's mother had often said in mild reproach, "but somehow never time to visit Gran in New Hampshire."

It seemed unfair that Melissa could go to Gran's now, when Mum couldn't.

"Fours Crossing!" called the conductor, opening the door to the nearly empty car where Melissa sat.

Melissa tried to peer out the window at the tiny village she hadn't visited since babyhood, but the snow was falling so much faster now that she had trouble seeing. There was nothing but white outside: white puffs of snow lining both sides of the frozen river, a snowy cluster of white houses with a church steeple rising in their midst; white roads, white branches of trees bent low with the snow's weight. Maybe when the sun was out it was pretty, the way Daddy said he remembered it from his boyhood, but right now it was even bleaker than Boston had been when she'd left it hours earlier.

Melissa stood up and struggled into her coat, tucking her long blond hair into the collar and pulling back the stray wisps that hung around her small, somewhat thin, but very determined-looking face. "It'll be fine, Pigeon; you'll love it — you'll see," Daddy had said as he'd kissed her goodbye. But she hadn't wanted to go. Even though Daddy was now only an unhappy ghost of himself, he was still Daddy, and he was all she had left of her mother. "He'll be better," Gran had written her, "after he's worked a bit again; I'm sure of it. Meanwhile, you come and keep me company; I could use some this snowy winter."

The old train's brakes hissed and then caught. Melissa walked to the back of the car and looked out at a platform so empty of people and so covered with unshoveled snow that she wondered for a moment if the train had stopped in the wrong place. Where was Gran? Where was a ticket agent, even, or a taxi driver?

There was no one in sight, no one at all, not even a stray dog sniffing along the icebound road or a wintertime bird perched on the snowy electrical wires.

The conductor swung Melissa's two suitcases down and looked doubtfully along the platform. "You sure your grandmother knows you're coming today?"

Melissa nodded numbly, wondering why she felt so calm, as if her fear were frozen — the way, she thought, looking around, Fours Crossing seems to be in all this snow.

"Well," said the conductor, tipping his hat and climbing up again, "there's a phone in the depot. Best you go and give your grandmother a call. Snow's so bad it might take her a while to get down the hill from her place."

Melissa thanked him, returning his wave as the train pulled out of the station. Then she realized that although the station building was only a few yards away, she could barely see it in the wildly blowing snow. She aimed herself toward the vague solid mass but halfway there she had to drop her suitcases and grab at her scarf, which had come loose in the wind and seemed to want to blow away. It was then that she saw a shape struggling onto the platform from the road — a boy, leaning back to keep from being blown into her as he approached. "You Melissa Dunn?" he gasped, red-faced with cold.

Melissa nodded. He was taller than she and seemed a bit older — maybe fourteen or fifteen. Unlike her, he was very dark, with earlobe-length hair spewing out from under his red knitted cap. The friendliness of his smile softened his somewhat angular face, and he spoke with an odd up-country twang that made him sound intriguingly old-fashioned. It wasn't an accent, really, just a choppier rhythm than the speech Melissa was used to, though he moved in a strong, relaxed way that wasn't choppy at all. "Your grandmother sent me to fetch you," he said, putting out a thickly mittened hand and shaking hers. "I'm Jethro Ellison." Before she could protest, he picked up her suitcases easily, as if he was used to carrying heavy loads. "Folks mostly call me Jed. Sorry I was late, but it's hard going in this snow." He looked with friendly disapproval at Melissa's ankle-length boots. "Those won't do you much good in all this," he said.

"I guess not," Melissa answered shyly. "But my father said the snow would be melting soon now that it's March. I never thought it would be this *deep*," she added, noticing that the snow seemed higher in spots than the station platform.

"Your dad grew up here, didn't he?" Jed asked.

Melissa nodded.

"Well, normally he'd be right about the melting." Jed led the way off the platform — and then put down her suitcases to pull her up from the drift she'd stumbled into. Cold wet snow dribbled down inside her boots. "But not this year. Snow's usually thinking about breaking up by now, squashing down anyway, but even your grandmother says she doesn't remember a winter as fierce as this one." He stopped abruptly and swung the suitcases up onto something far above Melissa's head, saying, "Hop in."

Melissa strained to see, took another couple of steps forward, and almost fell again, this time against a large, old-fashioned sleigh. "Oh!" she exclaimed, too delighted to hold back. "I didn't know people used sleighs any more!"

"Neither did any of us in Fours Crossing." Jed gave her a boost up a step into the sleigh and pulled himself up after her. "But this year everything's different. We were just lucky a couple of these old things were still around, and that we've still got a few horses who remember how to pull them. Gee-up!" he said, whacking reins against the back of a horse Melissa could barely see. With a lurch and a wonderful slidy sound, the sleigh moved forward. Bells jingled, and as Jed tossed her a red plaid blanket and told her to tuck it over her knees, Melissa caught herself thinking maybe she wasn't so sorry after all that she'd had to come to Fours Crossing.

It took about half an hour for Jed to drive the sleigh through the storm to Melissa's grandmother's. Melissa couldn't see much along the way, but she was sure they crossed the river again after somehow skirting the village proper, and that they spent a long time climbing a steep hill with snow-covered fields on each side of the road and only an occasional farmhouse. But finally, at the very top of the hill, Jed pulled up the horse and stopped.

"Here we are," he said cheerfully, and led Melissa along a path cut through shoulder-high snow. Melissa finally made out the outline of a smallish house ahead with soft yellow light shining through friendly windows.

Then a door opened, sending more light onto the snow, along with cooking smells and wood-smoke smells. "Is that you, Jed?" called a pleasant elderly voice. "Melissa?"

"Yes, Miz Dunn," Jed called back. "The train was late, and I was a mite later, but she's here now."

"Well, come in, children, out of the cold. Oh, Melissa . . ." And Melissa found her head buried in softness and felt herself clinging like someone much younger than thirteen.

Her grandmother gently pushed her back, holding her shoulders, and looked at her, smiling. Melissa saw tears in her eyes — blue-green eyes, merry and sad at the same time — and saw a short, square, comfortable body in a neat brown dress that didn't look grandmotherly, topped by a gray shawl that did.

"I shouldn't say you've grown," said Gran, her round face, weatherbeaten and wrinkled, made rounder by her broad smile, "but you have, and that's all there is to it." She patted her own ample body. "I daresay I have, too. And you look so much like your mother now that you're older! She was *such* a pretty woman."

"Thank you," said Melissa around the ache in her throat. She'd never thought of herself as pretty, exactly; in fact, ever since a year or so ago when she'd started caring more about how she looked,

7

she'd secretly thought her mouth much too large for her small face, her skin too pale, and her body hopelessly scrawny. But Mum — yes, Mum had been pretty, and if she grew up to look like her, it would make her feel proud.

"Well, come on in," Gran was saying. "You, too, Jed, for heaven's sake; you look as if you could do with some warming. Come in, Melissa, take off your things, come by the fire — here, this way. My, your coat is *covered* with snow, you poor child. Here, sit down."

Melissa, a little bewildered by all this bustling, found her coat suddenly off and herself as quickly settled in a large yellow wing chair in front of a cheerfully leaping fire. A small black-and-white cat blinked up at her from the hearth.

"I can't stay, Miz Dunn," Jed was saying from near the door, "but I'll take these cases up if you don't mind snow on your rugs. And I'll be by in the morning to take Melissa to school like you said and show her around."

"Well," said Gran, after she'd seen Jed upstairs and then out again, "here we are. Oh, you've met Pride and Joy, have you?" She nodded toward the cat, who uncurled itself and rubbed against Gran's ankles.

"Pride and Joy? Who are they?" asked Melissa.

Gran laughed and picked the cat up, plopping it down on Melissa's lap. "Just this beast," she said. "His mother had only one kitten — it was her first litter, if one's a litter — and she was so pleased with herself I named him Pride and Joy. Prudence's Pride and Joy; her name was Prudence."

8

Melissa smiled and scratched Pride and Joy behind the ears. Pride and Joy purred.

"He's good company," said Gran, turning a log in the fireplace, "especially since Prudence got run over last fall."

Melissa looked up, but her grandmother was still matter-of-factly poking the fire. Melissa gave Pride and Joy a private hug.

"Now then," said Gran, returning the poker and tongs to their rack. "How about some herb tea to warm you while I get supper ready?" She held a hand out to Melissa. "Come on out to the kitchen — there's a fire going there, too — while I fix you some."

The herb tea, which Gran made by steeping what looked like a lot of old twigs in hot water, looked thin but tasted delicious. Melissa sat at the heavy wooden table and drank two big mugs of it while Gran bustled around the kitchen and Pride and Joy slept on a red pillow at one corner of the ample brick hearth. The kitchen fireplace was even larger than the living-room one, and the kitchen itself reminded Melissa of one in a folk museum she and her parents had visited during one of Daddy's vacations. There were cooking pots hanging in neat rows along the walls, herbs and onions (one of which Gran now unbraided from its fellows and cut up) suspended in bunches from the rafters, and a big iron kettle on an iron bar over the center of the fieplace. But Gran's kitchen also had modern things like a copper-colored stove and refrigerator and a double aluminum sink under a wide window framed with red-and-white-checked curtains. There was also,

Melissa noticed, a rather battered bucket in the middle of the well-scrubbed wooden floor, into which water ominously dripped.

"Roof leaks," said Gran, turning to follow Melissa's glance. She popped the onion into a pot that steamed fragrantly on the stove. "It has for weeks, off and on. Mind you, roofs don't leak much up in this part of the world; they're built not to. But this winter — well, everything unusual that could happen *has* happened so far."

"Isn't it too cold for a leak?" asked Melissa.

"You're right, or nearly," said her grandmother. "But a lot of ice formed under the eaves in a couple of early storms, and the heat from the house melts it. Least that's what Jed's father says, and he ought to know. He's the best handyman around when he's steady — used to be a topnotch carpenter, but, poor man, he drinks a bit more than is good for him, as I suppose you'll see sooner or later." Gran went to the refrigerator and took out a bunch of carrots. "Jed's a fine boy, though," she said. "I hope you didn't mind my sending him to get you, 'stead of going myself, but . . ."

"No, no," said Melissa quickly. "He — he's nice. And it's so terrible out."

"It's the worst winter anyone's seen here for fifty years," said Gran, cutting carrots. "Maybe for longer. And the queer thing is . . ."

Gran's voice trailed off and she stopped cutting and gazed out the window into the growing darkness and the still-falling snow. She can't see a thing out there, thought Melissa, feeling suddenly uncomfortable; not a thing. Yet it looks as if she's seeing *something* . . .

"The queer thing is?" Melissa prompted.

"Oh, I don't know," said Gran quickly, vigorously going at the carrots, plopping them into the pot in little rounds. "Such nonsense. People get affected oddly by bad weather, that's all. Winter coops one up so. There," she said, putting the lid on the pot and turning down the electric burner. "I hope you like stew."

Melissa nodded, and while the stew cooked and the cat purred and the fire crackled, Gran set the table, talking quietly about Fours Crossing and the small village school Melissa would go to with Jed the next day.

"I used to teach there myself." Gran smiled, at last ladling out the stew. "Cooking and carpentry. I think the carpentry part embarrassed your father a little." She smiled. "But it was the most fun. All that practice at it has come in handy, too, especially since your grandfather died. Now eat up, child, before you fall asleep."

Sleepy as she was, Melissa had no trouble at all eating not only the stew and two big pieces of home-made bread but also a generous helping of baked custard topped with maple syrup, not to mention drinking another mug of herb tea. Afterward, though, it was all she could do to follow Gran up the narrow stairs to her room. She had a dim impression that it was tiny, tucked cozily under the eaves — near the chimney, Gran said, explaining why it was so warm. Melissa noticed that the walls were papered

11

in blue and white, that there was a full bookcase in one corner and a small desk with pencils and paper and a vase of blue and white dried flowers in another — and then she snuggled down under the warm patchwork quilt, switched off the bedside light, which looked like a kerosene lamp, and went to sleep.

It was halfway into morning before she had her usual dreams, but she had the whole cycle of them. They started with Mum laughing — only in the dream Melissa called her "Mumma," which had been her little-girl name for her. The dreams were like filmstrip pictures, one after the other: first Melissa and her mother bicycling on Boston Common, then riding swan boats in the Public Garden, looking in Filene's windows, eating ice cream at Brigham's. Melissa struggled to wake up, knowing what was coming, but she couldn't; the dream went relentlessly on: back to when she was tiny — her mother singing to her, reading to her; then to when she was older — Mum taking her to school, Mum sitting with her when she'd had her tonsils out, making her laugh . . . Then came the desolate feeling inside and the knot of fear again; the pictures came more quickly: Mum's face, so thin and pinched that her brave smile seemed too big for it; Mum's hair, gone white from X-ray treatments; her mind not always working, her words not always making sense; once, her crying uncontrollably and Melissa holding her, crying too. And then the dream went black and the hospital room turned to a barren winter graveyard and a deep hole cut into the dark and frozen ground.

Melissa woke drenched in sweat and pushed the covers off, biting her lip as always to keep from calling for her father. Then she remembered she was at Gran's, in all that snow, and Daddy was far away in Boston getting ready to drive west in the morning. She ached to cry, but knew from experience that no tears would come. "Be sensible," she told herself. "Stop dwelling on it, and go to sleep."

But she had to lie still for a long time, staring into the darkness and trying not to think, before sleep finally came.

By the time Melissa did sleep, the little village of Fours Crossing lay wrapped in profound silence, weighted heavily down by its cold thick layer of snow. Nothing stirred, not even the deeply buried snowdrops and crocuses that should by now have been stretching invisibly up through the ground toward spring.

Then at midnight a solitary dog strode softly out of the forest behind Gran's house, his long silky coat the color of palest gold. He walked straight to Gran's and stopped under Melissa's window, where he lay with great dignity on the unbroken snow till dawn, as if he were guarding something.

Or waiting.

2

By the next morning the snow had slowed to a few gently falling flakes, but all the trees and bushes were heavily frosted with white. Melissa saw from her bedroom window that far more snow lay on the ground than she had realized the night before. Billows buried walls and fences, mounds made roofless hallways out of roads. She couldn't help shivering as she dressed, though her room was warm; everything *looked* so cold.

Melissa was still trying to finish the thick oatmeal porridge Gran had made for breakfast when Jed came in from shoveling last night's snow off Gran's paths. "Don't know where I'm going to put it," he said to Gran, stamping snow off his boots, "if there's another big storm. Even the snow blowers are having trouble now. Hi, Melissa." Jed pulled two unmatched mittens off each hand and held hands and mittens

14

both out to the fire. "We'll have to hurry," he told her. "Mr. Coffin — that's the postman — needs the sleigh to deliver the mail. There'll be no cars driving today on most roads — both town plows are busted."

Melissa smiled at him as she put on the thick second sweater Gran handed her and struggled to button her coat over its bulk. Jed was so friendly and so matter-of-fact about having to take her to school that it was hard not to be friendly back.

"I've got some snowshoes for you down cellar," Gran said when Melissa was ready. "Once you get the knack of 'em, you'll be able to get to school on your own." She patted Melissa's shoulder. "Have a good day, lambie," she said, pushing them both gently out the door — and then closing it quickly.

Melissa could see why. The cold air hit her like air from the inside of a freezer. For the first few seconds she felt a stinging numbness, and then the warmth from the house left her body and the cold crept in, chilling first her skin, then her muscles, and at last her bones. The inside of her nose shrank away from the cold air as she breathed; her eyes ached and her whole body stiffened in protest.

"Pretty fierce, eh?" said Jed when they were both up in the sleigh. "It'll be better when you learn to snowshoe; you can keep moving then. Whack your arms around like this" — he demonstrated — "and you'll soon warm up."

They were early enough for Jed to give her a quick tour around the little town before pulling up in front of the three-story white frame house that served as the school. A house-lined circle marked the center of the village proper; three or four smaller roads

15

radiated out from it. A huge tower of snow rose out of the circle, with a flat space around it that could have been in a tiny park. "That's Bradford Ellison," Jed told Melissa when she stared at the tower, trying to figure out if it was just dumped snow or something more. "Well, a statue of him anyway, with" — Jed smiled — "with kind of a snowy coat on. He was the first minister in Fours Crossing, way back in seventeen-something-or-other. Very distant relation," he explained, as if he knew what Melissa, having noticed they had the same last name, was about to ask. He laughed. "About two centuries' worth of distance." He looked at her curiously. "You don't talk much, do you?"

Melissa shivered, even though it was less windy now that the sleigh had stopped. "I — I'm impressed," she said. "I don't know any famous Dunns."

Jed laughed and flicked the reins over the horse's back, starting him up again. "Lots of folks around here are named Ellison," he said. "It's nothing special. I bet Fours Crossing is the only town in the country where there are more *E*'s than *S*'s in the phone book. Did you ever notice that — that there are usually more *S*'s than anything else? Of course our town phone book's only ten pages long, small pages at that. There's the school," he said, steering the sleigh a quarter of the way around Bradford Ellison's little park. The white frame house he stopped at looked like most of the others except for being bigger. "Post Office is just across the green, with the general store next door. You can see the church right up there; the library's around back, in

16

the same building. There's no gas station, but there's a gas pump and an air hose at the store. You can buy almost anything there — food, fishing gear, farm stuff — well, most times you can. Sometimes lately deliveries haven't been able to get through. Last week they ran out of candy bars — the week before was the end of the six-penny nails." Jed took a deep breath and then made her laugh by saying, "No wonder you don't talk much! I don't give you a chance, do I? Well, your turn will come on the way home. You go in that door there — better hurry; I've been talking so much we're late. I guess you should go to the office first. It's to the left as you go in. Just tell them who you are and you'll be okay."

"Are — are they expecting me?" asked Melissa in a small voice.

"Sure. Your gran was down here last week setting it all up." His deep brown eyes probed hers for a second. "Don't worry," he said quietly, as if he understood. "They're okay. What grade are you? Seventh, isn't it?"

Melissa nodded. She found herself wishing she could wait for him, or deliver the sleigh with him so they could go in together. But of course she didn't have snowshoes and the snow did look too deep for boots — and it would be cold, waiting.

"I'm in eighth," said Jed, "so we'll be on the same floor. Just a few more months till I can go to the high school in Hiltonville — that's ten miles away." He gave her an awkward smile. "But I'll be here till June, so I guess I'll have time to show you around. I'll wait outside the seventh-grade room at

17

lunch, okay? Your teacher's all right, by the way. Her name's Miss Laurent and she's the daughter of the fire chief. You'll like her."

Melissa wondered how Jed could possibly know that, but he turned out to be right. She also liked the stout woman named Mrs. Ellison who showed her where the seventh-grade room was. "No direct relation to Jed," the woman told Melissa, after laughingly identifying herself as "the school secretary and, unless it's a broken arm or pneumonia or something like that, sort of the school nurse, too. Just watch out for frostbite. You'll need good warm clothes for a while yet, looks like, even if it *is* almost Spring Festival time."

Melissa was about to ask Mrs. Ellison what Spring Festival was, but Mrs. Ellison had already started up the stairs. The seventh-grade room was up two flights. After showing Melissa the girls' coat closet and bathroom, Mrs. Ellison opened the classroom door — and twenty pairs of eyes immediately turned toward Melissa and stared. She felt herself withdrawing again, even though this time she tried to smile.

Miss Laurent, who seemed to be halfway between young and old, looked up from the large book on her desk. She certainly had no trouble smiling. "Thank you, Mrs. Ellison," she said, and Mrs. Ellison said, "You'll be fine now," to Melissa, and left.

"Melissa," said Miss Laurent, "welcome to Fours Crossing. I'd get up, but . . ." She motioned with her head to a pair of crutches leaning against the blackboard behind her. "I was stupid enough to go

18

skiing alone last month and got a broken ankle for my foolishness."

Melissa couldn't see what being alone had to do with breaking one's ankle, but she said dutifully, "That's too bad, Miss Laurent."

"It certainly is," said Miss Laurent, "as everyone in this class knows, since they have to fetch and carry for me."

The class laughed good-naturedly, and that was when Melissa thought Jed was probably right about Miss Laurent.

"Class, this is Melissa Dunn from down in Boston," Miss Laurent said. "You remember I told you she was coming today."

Melissa wondered uncomfortably if Miss Laurent had also told them she was here because her mother had died, and if as a result they'd be curious about her or sorry for her.

"This is Joan Savage," Miss Laurent said, nodding toward a dark-haired girl in the front row. The girl got up as if she'd been told to in advance, and then quickly sat down again. She was very overweight, and looked embarrassed. "There's a seat for you right between Joan and Tommy Coffin. Tommy?"

A smallish boy with a friendly, open grin separating rows of freckles stood up as Melissa went to her seat. His face was a study in colors — brown freckles dotting white skin, red hair spilling out from under a green wool cap shaped like the top of an acorn, and, most startling of all, the green, yellow, and purple of a healing black eye blinking myopically at Melissa as she sat down.

"He wears that cap all the time," plump Joan

Savage whispered across the aisle. "It used to be Jed Ellison's, Tommy's next-door neighbor — Jed's in the eighth grade, and — well, he's sort of Jed's shadow. Or he'd like to be — I don't think Jed likes him hanging around much, but Tom's okay, really. He got that eye trying to beat up Tim Nickerson" — Joan wagged her head toward a tall brown-haired boy on the other side of Tommy — "for calling Jed's father a drunk. They're friends again now; Tommy and Tim, I mean."

Melissa smiled tentatively at Joan, finding all this a little too much to absorb as quickly as it was given to her, especially since Miss Laurent was rapidly running through all twenty seventh-grade names. Some of them were French-sounding, and, Melissa could see as well as hear, they were about evenly divided between boys and girls. Then Miss Laurent handed Melissa books and supplies, and finally returned to the social-studies lesson Melissa's arrival had obviously interrupted.

Melissa sank gratefully back into anonymity and stayed there until, during English (which had always been her worst subject), Tommy Coffin leaned over and whispered, "You look confused."

He seemed so eager to be friends that Melissa was startled out of her isolation into answering. "I hate English," she whispered back, "and I never did get those things she's talking about."

"Gerunds? Oh, they're easy, really. The thing is, they look like verbs but they're really nouns." Tommy smiled at her shyly. "Jed Ellison brought you to school, didn't he? Well, if he gets to be a — a friend of yours, you can ask him. He's good at

20

English — he even likes Shakespeare! He taught me gerunds."

"Oh," said Melissa, not knowing quite how to react.

Tommy glanced around at Miss Laurent, who seemed to be giving extra help to Tim Nickerson; Tim's forehead was wrinkled in concentration and he gnawed deeply at a pencil as Miss Laurent talked. "Gerunds," whispered Tommy, leaning across the aisle to Melissa, "like I said, they're really nouns. Um — if I said, 'They were fighting,' fighting's a verb, right? But if I said, 'Fighting gets you into trouble,' it's a noun — see?" He pushed up his cap and pointed to his black eye, winking the other one.

Melissa laughed.

"You should see the other guy," said Tommy, pointing with a twitch of his shoulder to Tim. "Oh, he looks okay on the outside, but I bet he won't be able to breathe out of his nose till Spring Festival, and that's a couple of weeks away."

Spring Festival again — but then the bell rang for lunch and Tommy poked Melissa; Jed had just appeared at the door.

When she and Jed were settled in the big lunchroom that covered almost the entire top floor, she asked him about it — and immediately wondered if she'd said something wrong. But he did answer, after giving her a startled glance over the top of his milk carton and then carefully putting it down. When he spoke, it was in a faraway voice at first, as if he were reading out of a book, and he was hesitant, as if he were skipping bits here and there.

"Spring Festival," he said carefully, "is a very

21

old custom. It's on March twenty-first or whenever the equinox is — the first day of spring, anyway. This year it's March twenty-first. But this year . . ." He broke off for a moment, then shook his head as if to rouse himself from a dream or a thought he didn't want to think. "Well, anyway. It's an old custom, with a procession and singing, things like that. It — it's supposed to bring spring, or welcome it, depending on how you look at it. The little kids all think it brings it. They believe in it like they believe in Santa Claus. The procession . . ."

Melissa heard a clatter at her elbow and Tommy Coffin appeared, slapping his metal lunch box onto the table. "Hi," he said, glancing quickly at Jed and then smiling at Melissa. "Spring Festival, huh?" He pulled out a chair and sat down between them. "Hey, Melissa, Festival's really neat — you'll love it, I bet, won't she, Jed? See, everyone goes into the woods the night before — well, early in the morning, really, while it's still dark — and cuts down this tree just about at sunrise, and then everyone comes back here and there's a procession from house to house with singing — like I said, it's neat!"

Jed crumpled his empty lunch bag, his face oddly troubled. "It may seem — backward to you," he said to Melissa, "or superstitious, coming from the city and all. But the procession starts and ends at your gran's house . . ."

"Yes," interrupted Tommy, "that ought to make it special for you!" He opened his lunch box, lifting out a thermos and several large foil packages. "Man," he said, unwrapping a huge sandwich, "I sure can't wait for Spring Festival this year, can you, Jed?

Want some sandwich? No? Well, I can't wait. I've had just about all the winter I think I'm ever going to want! You see, Melissa, there's always a thaw right after, or almost right after, and . . ." .

"We hope there's a thaw," Jed said, frowning. He tossed his crumpled lunch bag accurately into a small trash can halfway across the room. "We *hope*."

3

Some snow fell every day that first week Melissa spent in Fours Crossing, but luckily it added up to no more than an inch or so on top of what was already on the ground. Both plows were fixed by Wednesday, so the roads could be opened again, but it was Thursday before the general store had bakery bread or fresh milk from dairies outside Fours Crossing. There were still no candy bars, and Melissa secretly stopped using the old-fashioned cocoa-butter ointment Gran gave her for her chapped face, because Jed said its smell made him hungry.

Despite the odd way he'd acted that first day at lunch, Jed was rapidly becoming her best Fours Crossing friend. Tommy and Joan were nice enough, and Tim was, too, but Jed was special. He didn't seem to have any other friends, except of course for Tommy, who followed him around like a puppy; sometimes that annoyed Jed so much he snapped at the younger boy. That wasn't true when it came to Melissa, though; in fact, Jed seemed so glad to be with her most of the time that on Saturday, when she was helping Gran polish silver, Melissa was startled to learn that Gran hadn't been sure they'd get along. "I was worried," Gran said. "You're so much alike. It looked like a toss-up between your being standoffish with each other and your being good for each other." She smiled. "Looks like the last, so I'm glad I gambled!"

"How are we alike?" Melissa asked curiously, spreading polish on a small tray.

Gran put down the teapot she'd been working on and looked thoughtfully outside to where her back field stretched to a stone wall and ended in thick, dark woods. "Well," she said finally, "it's his place, not mine, to tell you about himself. But I guess he won't, so I'll say this. He's lonely, like you, lambie — no brothers or sisters, and his mother died when he was small. I think that troubles him sometimes as much as his father's drinking — which I probably shouldn't have mentioned, Melissa, but I did think I ought to warn you in case you see him some time. Jed doesn't talk about his troubles much until they boil over." Gran rinsed the teapot. "I guess that's how you're alike." She smiled again. "Sometimes I think you're even quieter than he about what's bothering you."

Melissa was dimly aware that Gran seemed to be questioning her, even though she was talking about Jed — but she was still stuck back on her words "lonely, like you" and "his mother died when he was small."

25

"Some folks don't agree," Gran said, shaking water off the teapot, "but I always think it's best to talk troubles out. After your grandfather died — well, at first I didn't want to say anything to anybody about him or about how it had been with us; I wanted to keep him all to myself. I think I was also scared that if I talked too much, I'd start crying and never stop. But not talking got lonely, too, and when I finally did, I felt better. Talking even made him seem closer, somehow."

Gran glanced at Melissa as if inviting her to speak, but when Melissa didn't — couldn't — she sighed and reached up to the rack above her head for a dish towel.

"There," she said when the teapot was dry, "we're through. A good morning's work, I'd say." Gran groped in the sink for the stopper but then pulled her hand out again, shaking the water off it. "We're not through, either," she said. "I forgot the plates — might as well put a shine on them now for Spring Festival. Would you get them, Melissa — the big silver plates from the dining-room wall?"

Melissa got up willingly, so glad for the change in subject she decided to get the plates first and then ask Gran what they could possibly have to do with a festival that seemed to take place outside, not indoors, where one would expect plates to be. Besides, she was also glad of the excuse to go into the dining room again. She'd seen it only once before — Gran kept it closed in winter to save fuel — but it was her favorite room in Gran's house, next to her own.

She opened the side door and was immediately dazzled with brightness, for the white beamed ceiling and whitewashed walls picked up and reflected the least bit of light from outside. One wall framed a huge bright-colored tapestry that Gran said her own grandmother had made. Tiles, trivets, and plaques were arranged in careful abandon on another wall, along with an antique candle snuffer, and on each side of a stone fireplace, a pair of three-dimensional carved pictures of houses so real you could certainly live in them if you could make yourself small enough. There was also a shelf of fragile teacups, all different; an old-fashioned spoon rack filled with souvenir spoons from all over the world — and, best of all, the three large silver plates Gran had asked for.

They hung in a triangle facing the window, the third beneath and between the other two. A pale space showed that a fourth plate had once hung above the others, making the complete group form a diamond — or a square, or even a large circle. Each plate was about ten inches across, with a wide, heavily carved border. That was ordinary enough, but the curious thing was the L-shaped groove cut into the center of each, making the plates look a little like the divided ones sometimes given to babies so their mothers can keep their vegetables from running into their meat.

Carefully, Melissa lifted the plates down and stacked them, not surprised to find that they were quite heavy. Then she carried them into the kitchen, where she put them down on the table.

"I usually shine the plates up for Spring Festival," said Gran, answering Melissa's question before Melissa asked it, "since the procession stops right ouside the window and people can see in. Usually open up the dining room, too, but it's been so cold and dreary I don't think I will this year." Gran pointed to Pride and Joy, who was lying on the table. "Better get him down. Although goodness knows, the plates are probably too heavy for him to harm."

Melissa gave Pride and Joy a gentle push and sat down so she could examine the plates more closely.

The patterns on their borders looked like leaves or twining branches at first. But then, as Melissa studied them, she saw there was a section in each that reminded her of letters, though not of any letters she had ever seen:

"They're so pretty," Melissa said, running her finger over the decorations on the border of one plate. "Don't you ever use them?"

"I never have," Gran said, coming over to the table. "And I'm not sure anyone else has either." She picked up a plate and pointed to its L-shaped groove. "I daresay they'd be a pain to wash — food would stick in here, and they're really too pretty, as you say." She carried the heavy plate to the sink and dunked it carefully in water preparatory to polishing it. "I'm not sure they're even *for* eating," she said, "though heaven knows what they are for if not that. They've always been here, you know — they came with the house and always hung on that wall, or so your great-grandfather always said." Gran paused, swishing the plate absently back and forth in the water as if she were more intent on what she was saying than what she was doing. "The dining room's the original house, you know. It was built back in the 1670s — the first house in the village. In fact, the village itself was the first settlement in these parts — the only one, too, for a long time. The rest of the house was added on later in bits and pieces, but the plates were in the original part from the beginning. I don't know where they came from before that — I suppose Scotland, with the first Dunns. There used to be four of them — plates, I mean, but I'm sorry to say one was stolen a while back when I was in Hiltonville getting my eyes examined." Gran took the plate out of the sink and began rubbing it with polish. "I'm not even sure they're all that valuable, but of course they're antique silver, so they must be worth something." She put the plate down reverently. "They're worth more than money, though, dear old things that they are."

"No one ever caught the thief?" Melissa asked.

"No. Oh, the police tried, all right, but whoever he was, he left no sign of himself, not even fingerprints. The odd thing was that there was nothing to show he'd gone into any other room but the dining room, or hunted for jewelry or anything." Gran laughed. "Not that there's much to take anyway in this house," she said. "One wonders why anyone would bother to break in at all."

Melissa looked again at the borders of the two

29

plates that were still on the table, and followed the patterns with her finger. "They do look mostly like leaves," she said, fascinated, "but then there are the extra un-leafy squiggles on each one. I wonder if it *is* writing."

"I used to wonder, too," said Gran, bringing back the polished plate and picking up another. "The squiggles do look like letters, don't they?"

Melissa frowned as she studied them squiggle by squiggle. But before she'd finished there was a faint jingle of sleigh bells outside and Gran, glancing at the clock, said, "Mr. Coffin's early with the mail for a Saturday. Would you go out and get it, Melissa?"

Melissa gave the plates one last look and pulled on her boots and jacket, reluctant to go till she realized that by now there might be a letter from her father.

The sky looked grayer than it had earlier. Melissa had never actually seen Gran's small outdoor mailbox, for it was buried in snow with only the opening kept clear. "The mail," she had written her father, "is delivered into a snowdrift, and each time it snows hard, Gran says, she has to dig the mailbox door out again." Thinking of that, Melissa leaned around the shoveled edge of the drift — and suddenly froze, her hand poised in midair, reaching for the mail.

Standing in the road staring at her was a large pale-gold dog with gold-brown eyes — eyes with yellow flecks, with blue flecks, with green and possibly red flecks, too; eyes that stared so intensely up into hers that for a moment Melissa couldn't move.

How foolish, she thought. It's only a dog.

But she knew dogs rarely stare like that; few can look for any time at all right into a person's eyes.

30

"Nice dog," Melissa said tentatively, trying to stay calm, and annoyed that her mouth had gone dry and that her heart was pounding as if in fear. Slowly, she moved her hand toward the dog so he could sniff it. "Nice boy, good boy."

For what seemed like forever, the dog didn't move. They both stood there motionless, facing each other, Melissa with her hand out till it began to ache. Then at last the dog touched her hand delicately, almost politely, with his nose, and with great solemnity held up one front paw.

Melissa laughed softly in relief. "Good dog," she said, relaxed now. "Nice dog. You want to shake hands, right?"

She took his paw and the dog let her, but though his tail wagged slightly, brushing like a furry branch against the hard-packed snow in the road, he gave her such a look of indulgent patience she was sure she had misunderstood; he hadn't meant her to shake his paw at all.

But of course, she told herself, that's silly, too. What else does a dog want when he holds out his paw? Unless it's to be patted . . .

"Melissa?" called Gran from the house. "You fall into a drift?"

"No, I'm okay," Melissa called back, turning toward the house. "Look, Gran, I found the funniest dog out here — oh, but you can't see around the drift, can you?" Melissa turned to try and coax the dog onto the path — but the dog was no longer there.

In fact, there was no sign of him at all, not even tracks in the snow.

31

But of course, she reassured herself as she took in the mail — there was only a brief postcard from her father — the snow's too hard in the road today for tracks . . .

"I bet it's the stray," Jed said the next afternoon when Melissa told him about the dog. "People have been seeing one around for the last week or so — a big yellowy one, like you said. Just about since you got here," he added, looking at her curiously as he lifted another log. They were in Gran's cellar re-arranging her woodpile, and Jed was trying to figure out if she had enough wood to last till warm weather. He straightened up. "Your gran does need more. She can't get through till spring with just this. Whenever spring is," he muttered, reaching for the last log and adding it to the pile. "Funny, we're all still talking around here as if it were the middle of January, not March and close to Spring Festival. I keep thinking it's as if time had stopped, or something."

He went to the window in the upper part of the cellar door and looked out. The door was below ground level, not up steps the way the back door was; all but its top five inches was buried in snow. A few new flakes were falling lazily. "I wonder if time *has* stopped," Jed said softly, watching them drift down. "I wonder if that could be what's gone wrong . . ."

"Are you serious?" asked Melissa. She wondered briefly if he might be joking, but something in his face when he turned back told her he wasn't.

"Half," Jed answered. Then he laughed. "Oh, that's dumb," he said, shrugging it off. "It does something to the mind, all this snow. Come on — let's get your gran some more wood before it gets any worse out."

It was hard work, slogging through the still unbroken snow in the woods, helping Jed pull the sled with its heavy load of two saws and a hatchet. Melissa found that she had to watch carefully where she stepped with her snowshoes and that she couldn't look around much — only enough to see that most of the trees on both sides of them were hemlocks, and that the bottom branches of many were so heavy with snow they touched the ground, forming cozy little tents for animals to hide under. There were all kinds of light tracks around the trees, but no real paths anywhere that Melissa could see. There were no bird sounds either, once they'd left the stone wall and the forest rapidly thickened.

"Just up here," panted Jed after around twenty more minutes. "There are some regular trees soon — you know, the kind that lose their leaves in the fall. We'll find a few partway down, I hope, and we can fell them the rest of the way and saw them small enough to fit on the sled. They burn better than hemlock." He looked at her. "Not scared, are you?"

"N-no," she said, "not exactly. It's just that it's awfully dark in here. And quiet. Even though it *is* pretty."

"I know," he said. "I was scared to go into these woods alone myself till just a couple of years ago. There's an old hermit living here — oh, not where we'll be, unless . . ." He grinned. "Unless you want to pay a call on him." Melissa shook her head.

"People used to say terrible things about him — that he's a wizard, that he eats kids — you know the kinds of things people say."

Melissa shivered as some snow slid off a branch onto her face, but she kept still.

"Anyway," called Jed as he stomped ahead, pulling the sled behind him, "he lives farther than we're going, beyond the regular trees in another hemlock section with pines beyond. Come on, we'd better hurry; it's snowing harder."

Melissa wondered how they would find their way out again if the falling snow covered their tracks, but she didn't ask. Jed did seem to know the way into the woods; she'd just have to believe he could find the way out, too.

In a few minutes the sky seemed to get lighter, and then they came out of the dark hemlocks into what seemed to be a clearing. It wasn't, because there were still deciduous trees all around — "regular trees," as Jed had called them. Their leafless branches let in considerably more light than had the evergreen hemlocks.

Jed stooped, untying the saws, and then pointed to a medium-sized tree that leaned out of the snow at an angle. "Dead, most likely," he said. "I'm going to try cutting some of the branches off first."

Melissa watched as Jed reached partway up the trunk and started sawing at a thick branch. When the cut was about halfway through, he stopped and unzipped his jacket. "Whew!" he said. "Your turn. That wood's harder than I thought."

Melissa took the second saw from the sled, trying to hold it as Jed had, but she could only reach the branch with the tip of the saw. Jed burst out laughing.

"What's so funny?" she asked, dropping her arm, mad.

"I'm not laughing at you," he said, picking up his saw again. "I'm laughing at me. I'm sorry. I guess you just don't seem as short as you are. You can't possibly saw at that angle — I started too high for you." He began sawing again.

Melissa stopped being angry, mostly, but she still didn't like being reminded she couldn't do something he could, even if it wasn't her fault. She took the other saw and clumped away from Jed till she spotted another leaning tree.

Then, just as she reached up to a branch that was at a comfortable sawing height for her, she saw the dog again, sitting like a pale-gold ghost in the snow only a few feet away.

Melissa stood absolutely still, but the big dog solemnly held out his paw the way he had before. The tip of his tail twitched on the snow, and his eyes, although they still looked mysterious, were friendly.

"Hello," Melissa said softly, taking the paw and stroking it this time instead of shaking it. It looked silky, like the rest of the dog's pale coat, but of course she couldn't really tell with gloves on. "Why do you have to appear like that?" she asked, as if she almost expected an answer. "Couldn't you just trot up to people the way most dogs do?"

The dog cocked his head and whined.

"Who're you talking to . . . Melissa?" called Jed from farther away than Melissa thought she'd gone; it was odd, how distances seemed to increase more quickly here in the forest than they did back in the village.

"Here I am, Jed," she called, still softly. "It's that dog again."

She heard the muffled crunch of Jed's snowshoes, and then he was beside her, the sled, partly loaded now, behind him and his saw over one shoulder.

"Hello, dog," he said matter-of-factly, squatting down. "You're a strange one, aren't you?"

The dog solemnly held out his paw again, and Jed took it. Still holding it, he reached up to a collar Melissa hadn't noticed before. Then he gave a long, low whistle. "Wow," he said, "someone sure cares about you, dog, don't they?" He held the collar away from the dog's neck so Melissa could see.

It was made of three thin, rope-like golden strands braided together, brighter than the dog's coat but the same color. A small gold tag danced against Jed's hand. Even on this gray day with snow lazily falling, the gold sparkled.

"Let's have a look at that tag," said Jed. "Doesn't look like a license. You a stray, dog?"

The dog grunted and stretched his neck out as if he wanted to help Jed see his tag.

"U-L-F-I-N," Jed spelled out. "There's just a design on the back, but the front says Ulfin. That your name, boy?"

The dog jumped up and barked, wagging his tail vigorously — for the first time since she'd seen him, Melissa realized. He nuzzled both their hands.

"Okay." Jed laughed. "I guess it is. Ulfin — right, dog?" The dog wagged his tail harder. "Ulfin. What a weird name."

"Look, Jed," said Melissa. "I think he wants us to follow him."

37

Ulfin was prancing ahead of them now, lively as a puppy. He ran back every few steps, nuzzling and pushing them both but especially Melissa, before leaping forward again.

Jed glanced up at the sky; the snow was falling a little faster. "I think he wants us to follow him, too," he said, "but I don't like the look of that sky."

"He's right," Melissa told herself; "be sensible." But curiosity told her to follow. Suppose Ulfin's master were lying unconscious somewhere alone in the woods, hurt and freezing? Suppose the dog knew where there were lost children, a sick old woman, stranded sheep?

"I think we ought to go, Jed. He really wants us to."

Sighing, Jed strapped his saw back onto the sled. "I guess the sled's heavy enough now to make tracks," he said dubiously, shifting the wood around on it. "I guess we'll be able to follow them home. But we can't go far, Melissa; it's snowing harder and our tracks will be covered soon."

"Look," said Melissa, pointing. "Look at the tracks Ulfin's leaving."

The dog, who didn't look heavy enough even though he was large, was now making deep paw prints in the snow as he ran ahead of them, paw prints so deep a blizzard would be needed to cover them.

"Odd," said Jed, looking back to where they'd been. "He didn't leave any tracks getting here that I can see. Now suddenly he's making huge ones."

"He didn't leave any on the road yesterday,

either," said Melissa slowly. She watched the dog with a growing feeling of discomfort. There was definitely something not quite real about him, despite the dog-like way he was prancing back and forth and urging them to follow; something magical about his pale-gold coat and his bright-gold collar, his strange name and his even stranger way of appearing out of nowhere . . .

Be sensible, Melissa.

"Look at the way he's jumping," said Jed. "Maybe that's why his tracks are suddenly so deep."

Melissa forced herself to watch with what she hoped was proper scientific detachment — much better, she thought, to try to analyze the problem than worry about it and imagine all sorts of silly things. "Yes," she said, "that must be it. He's jumping so high that he sinks in when he lands." But she didn't mention to Jed that by now she had also noticed he didn't jump with every step, and that the tracks he left looked just as deep when he didn't jump as when he did.

Ulfin led them to a lumpily buried stone wall at the far edge of the grove of deciduous trees. Beyond the wall there were hemlocks again, only these were truly dark and forbidding, much closer together than the ones right behind Gran's.

"You don't want us to go in there, do you, old boy?" Jed asked the dog.

Ulfin pranced around him, lifting his front legs high like a spirited horse. Then he jumped over the wall and turned and barked at them, tail still wagging.

"I think he does," said Melissa.

"That old hermit lives some place in there," said Jed. "I'd sure hate to disturb him."

"The one you said all those stories are about?"

"Right. Eating kids. That kind of story."

"Oh, Jed. Hermits don't eat kids."

Jed laughed suddenly, his clear voice ringing out in the frosty air. "No," he said a little crazily. "They don't. Kids eat hermits — the kind with raisins in them."

Melissa laughed, too, visualizing a cookie-shaped person with raisins for eyes. Immediately Ulfin jumped back over the wall and jumped on them both, licking their faces and making them laugh more. Then, just as Melissa thought all he really wanted was to have them play with him, he prodded her sharply and suddenly with his nose. He nipped her thigh and then Jed's, stunning them both into silence.

Melissa felt a chill that had nothing to do with the cold. She moved away from the dog and they both stared at him.

He was sitting very straight and quietly, his slowly wagging tail making a single snow angel wing in the snow. He looked from one to the other of them, alert and friendly as before, as if nothing had happened.

"Did he hurt you?" asked Jed.

Melissa shook her head. "He just got my pants. You?"

"Same thing. Melissa . . ."

"Let's go home," said Melissa.

"Good." Jed turned — but Ulfin growled and swiftly blocked his path.

I am not going to be scared, Melissa said to herself. Ulfin's only a dog. I like dogs . . .

"Out of the way, Ulfin," commanded Jed.

Ulfin snarled, baring his teeth this time.

"Holy cow," said Jed under his breath. "I think he means it."

Melissa, pushing her fear under, squatted as best she could on her snowshoes and held out her hand to Ulfin. He stopped snarling right away and nuzzled her, wagging his tail and becoming, all over again, an ordinary friendly, floppy dog. Carefully Melissa stood up and tried to go past him; instantly he sprang in front of her, snarling.

"I think he means it, too," she said. She tried not to notice that there was a wind coming up and that the snow was falling faster, that their own tracks had disappeared along with the sled's and that, though Ulfin's tracks were still visible, even they were fast being obliterated. "We'd better go his way," she said reluctantly. "Maybe if we hurry we'll find whatever he wants us to find before the snow gets much deeper."

"I don't see how we can *not* go with him," said Jed, "but . . ." He shook his head. "Well," he said, obviously trying to sound cheerful, "we've got plenty of wood, and I've got matches — I hope." He rummaged in his pockets. "Yup. And I've got my knife, and we've got the saws and the hatchet. We won't freeze, anyway. As for food . . ."

Melissa took the sled rope from him. She didn't have so much as a cracker and she was sure he didn't either. The last thing she wanted was to think about what would happen if they got lost for very long or if Ulfin led them into bad trouble. She just wanted to get it over with, whatever it was. "Okay, Ulfin," she said. "Go on, boy, we're ready."

Tail held high and jauntily, Ulfin jumped over the wall and ran into the hemlock forest. Melissa and Jed plodded after him under the dark trees, dislodging little plops of snow as they brushed against low-hanging branches. "Oh, rats!" Jed exclaimed in a whisper after about ten minutes of silent walking, "I think he's taking us to the hermit's place. Oh, holy cow. Melissa, look!"

Ulfin had stopped and was crouching, his eyes intent on something ahead. Melissa heard what sounded like the voice of an elderly man, half singing, half chanting. Jed grabbed her arm and both of them dropped to their stomachs behind Ulfin, staring.

Ahead was a clearing, and in the clearing was a small, tumbledown, grayish-brown house. Two pairs of loose shutters in front were fastened with a tangle of rope and wire over two small high windows. The front door was more firmly closed, but it was made out of so many different shapes and kinds of boards that Melissa couldn't tell what it had looked like when it had been new — a long time ago, she guessed, not only from the rest of the house's dilapidated appearance but also from its large central chimney, from which snaked a thin curl of gray smoke.

Outside, a bit to one side of the door, was a heap of half-buried gray planks that might once have been some sort of shed, and nearby, sticking up every which way out of the snow, was an amazing assortment of junk: old bedsprings, gardening tools, pots and pans. It was obvious to Melissa that only the tops of the many junk piles were visible; she thought of icebergs and was sure there was far more under the snow.

In the middle of the clearing, where it looked as if a space had been shoveled for it, was an upright trio of sticks, criss-crossed to form a tripod.

"It's the hermit's place all right," Jed whispered. "And it sure looks as if he's been working harder than usual at raiding the town dump." He pointed at one of the piles, where the handle of what must once have been a lawnmower made a black *T* against the snow.

Ulfin pressed himself close between Jed and Melissa; Melissa was startled to feel his body shaking and put an arm around him to comfort him. He licked her face gratefully and then stared ahead into the clearing, his nose and ears twitching with excitement.

"Look at Ulfin," Jed whispered unnecessarily. "It's as if he's waiting for something." He turned as if to get up and go back the way they'd come. But Ulfin leaped in front of him, growling softly.

"Okay, boy, okay." Jed patted him and settled back facing the clearing. "We understand, okay. This is where you want us. But what do you want us to do? We can't sit here forever."

"I think," Melissa whispered, "that he'll probably lead us home when he's through with us."

Jed looked doubtful, but he didn't say anything.

Melissa said nothing more either, and they all huddled there quietly, like three frozen statues in the snow.

It got colder, and the snow fell faster, and there was no sound except for, now and then, the faint odd chanting from somewhere behind the partly shuttered windows. Melissa gave up trying to make words out of the chant; it seemed to be a foreign language or maybe just run-together sounds or nonsense words repeated over and over again. She no longer felt cold; she was even beginning to feel comfortable if not quite warm, and after a while, lulled by what they could hear of the chant, she began to feel pleasantly sleepy.

Just as her eyes drooped shut, a sharp jab from Jed's elbow roused and nearly toppled her. If she hadn't been almost asleep she would have cried out, but luckily she didn't. Out of the house, carrying something beneath the long black cloak he wore, came the oddest figure Melissa had ever seen. She had to blink her eyes and rub them with her half-frozen glove and blink again to make sure she was really seeing what she thought she was seeing.

"The hermit," whispered Jed. "Holy cow."

Melissa stared.

He looked like a magician out of a child's storybook — tall, wrinkled, with a long white beard and white bushy eyebrows. Even at the distance she was from him Melissa could see his black eyes snap coldly as they darted around the clearing, as if he sensed someone was hidden there watching him. She shuddered and tried to hunch down further into the snow.

The black cloak's long sleeves hid the hermit's arms but not his hands, which were ungloved and gnarled, with long yellowed nails curling over the

44

tops of his fingers like claws. He was lifting them now, those old and withered hands, raising something that so far was hidden by his flowing sleeves — raising it higher and higher above his head, still chanting as he walked slowly toward the tripod of sticks.

Then he slowly brought the object down. He balanced it carefully on the top of the tripod and stepped back.

Melissa gasped.

It was the fourth plate.

The fourth silver plate from her grandmother's dining-room wall.

5

"Okay," said Jed when they were safely back at Gran's and Ulfin had disappeared into the forest as silently as he'd come to them. "The first thing is, why does the hermit have the plate — did he steal it himself or did he just find it some place? And the second thing is, how do we get it back?"

"And the third thing," said Melissa, "is what does that dog have to do with it?"

"The fourth thing," said Gran firmly, coming into the kitchen, where Jed and Melissa were warming themselves by the fire, "is when are you going to call your father, Jed, to tell him you're staying here for the night?"

Jed looked at her in disbelief. "The night?" he asked stupidly. "What do you mean? You know how he is, Miz Dunn, he . . ."

"I know how it is outside, young man," Gran said. "The visibility out there is zero and the temperature's close to the same, and there's a mean fierce wind coming up. Now, march!"

Sheepishly, Jed padded out to the hall in his socks — his boots still lay in puddles on Gran's inside doormat — and Melissa could hear him dialing.

"Gran," said Melissa, starting to tell her about the plate — but Gran held up her hand and nodded toward the hall. Jed was obviously having trouble communicating with his father on the phone.

"At Miz Dunn's," he was shouting. "No — Dunn — on the hill — you know, Dad — NO, DUNN!" He shot a glance at Gran, and Melissa was horrified to see that he was nearly in tears. "I can't make him understand, Miz Dunn," he said. "He — he's pretty far gone, I guess. I guess I'd better go on home."

"Just let me have that telephone," Gran said crisply.

Jed handed it to her.

Melissa tried to make a lot of noise filling the kettle. She was pretty sure Jed wouldn't want her to have noticed his almost-tears.

"Seth Ellison, you listen to me. Janet Dunn — *Janet*, you old reprobate, J-A-N-E-T . . ."

Jed grinned, so Melissa felt it was all right now to smile at him.

". . . and I'm not sending that poor boy of yours out in this raging snowstorm. He'll be here till it stops, probably for the night, you hear? . . . Oh, for heaven's sake, NO!"

Jed laughed nervously and Melissa joined him, wondering what the NO! was for.

"You just keep yourself warm, Seth, and Jed'll be home tomorrow. You got plenty of wood? . . . WOOD! . . . Well, fine then, you just stay inside by the fire." Gran hung up after a quick goodbye, and shook her head. "I think he understood, Jed," she said, "but just in case, I'd better walk down with you tomorrow."

"Oh, that's okay," he said gruffly. "He'll probably have such a head tomorrow he won't even notice I've been gone."

"He *will* be all right, won't he?" Gran asked.

"Oh, sure. Tommy Coffin's folks next door keep an eye on him, anyway. Maybe I'll give them a call, though, just to make sure they know I'm not home."

Jed went back into the hall, and Gran, filling a large saucepan at the sink, said, "Melissa, just run down cellar, would you, please, and bring up the canner? I have a feeling we'd better draw some water in case the power goes off in this storm."

"*Draw* water?" Melissa asked, giggling.

Gran smiled. "It does sound funny, doesn't it? Must be left over from when water came from a well. It still does here, you know, but an electric pump brings it up, which is why we have to . . ."

The kitchen was suddenly plunged into darkness except for the glow from the fireplace, where Pride and Joy sat placidly washing his face.

". . . draw water before power failures," finished Gran wryly. She put the full saucepan down on the counter. "Well, we've got this, anyway. And the kettle."

"Guess it's a good thing I'm staying," Jed remarked, groping his way back into the room. "Where's your kerosene, Miz Dunn?"

"Lamps are filled already. You might bring in the big one from the living room — here's a flashlight. And, Melissa, there are some candles in that drawer right by you."

When the candles were lit and Jed had trimmed the wick of the kerosene lamp and lit it, too, Gran asked Melissa and Jed to set the table, and they didn't get around to telling her about the plate till after dinner. They couldn't use the electric stove, of course, so they cooked in the big iron kettle over the fireplace — two cans of milky chowder with canned minched clams added. With it they had a hefty loaf of Gran's dark whole-wheat bread, baked that morning and warmed in the little oven built into the side of the fireplace.

Then, sitting around the kitchen table, their faces touched with gold light from the kerosene lamp, they listened to the blizzard rage outside and told Gran about the hermit and her fourth plate.

"It was as if he was doing some kind of ceremony with it," Jed said, describing the hermit's lifting the plate above the tripod. "Some kind of mysterious thing . . ."

"And the words he chanted didn't even sound like words," put in Melissa. "Not English ones, anyway."

Gran frowned, and sipped her tea. "That old hermit's always been a bit odd," she said, "but he's perfectly harmless, as far as anyone knows. He's a Dunn, too, you know, Melissa, though you'd never guess it for all he's kept to himself all these years."

49

"You mean we're related to him?" Melissa asked excitedly. "You mean I am?"

"Well, yes," said Gran. "I suppose he's some kind of cousin of yours, many times removed, or whatever they call it." She laughed. "I never could keep that sort of thing straight." She took a swallow of tea and put her cup down. "To get back to the plate, though, I guess I'd just as soon let the hermit keep it, odd as that may sound. I *am* relieved to know where it is — but after all, it's still in the family — and I suppose in a way he has more right to it than I do, since he was born into the family like you, Melissa, and I only married into it. Besides," she went on, sipping her tea again, "I don't want to make trouble for the poor old man. If the police knew he had the plate, they'd have to investigate, and then goodness knows what would happen. Somehow I can't believe old Eli John — that's the hermit's name — I can't believe he'd break in here, or anywhere else for that matter. My guess is that someone else took the plate and then threw it away at the dump — maybe it wasn't as valuable as they thought — and old Eli John found it."

"How come he lives all by himself like that?" Melissa asked curiously. "It must be awful!"

Gran had started collecting bowls and cups, but she stopped when Melissa asked her question. "I suppose it *is* lonely for him," she said, "but some folks like being by themselves. And, as I said, Eli John's always been a bit odd. He always kept to himself, even as a boy — barely went to school and never went to church. He was always off by himself in the woods, ever since I can remember, so no one was too surprised when he went there — oh, maybe forty years ago — to live in the old Keeper's House, as everyone used to call it."

"The Keeper's House?" Melissa asked. "You mean that old tumbledown thing has a name?"

"Well, it did once." Gran smiled. "Everyone around here knows the story so well, what there is of it, anyway, that I almost forgot it'd be new to you. But you're family, and of course you should know it — if Jed doesn't mind hearing it again."

Jed shook his head.

"There was some trouble years back," Gran began, after passing around a plate of homemade doughnuts and pulling her sweater more closely around her. "Oh, *many* years ago, I mean, way back at the beginning of Fours Crossing. The Dunns were town elders then, you might say, and their leader was also named Eli. I suppose our hermit, Eli John, was named after him; most of the Elis in the family were. The original Eli was the one who led the first settlers here back in the late 1600s and he was also the one who built the beginnings of this house . . ."

"The dining room," said Melissa, remembering.

"Where the plates hang," Jed put in suddenly, as if something aside from the story had just struck him. "Holy cow! I wonder . . ."

But then he fell silent, and Gran, after a moment, went on.

"Yes, and I guess it was he who hung the plates here, too. Well," Gran continued, "after a number of years a minister — Bradford Ellison, the one whose statue you've seen in the village, Melissa, and who's distantly related to Jed — Bradford Ellison

51

came up from Massachusetts Bay Colony, and, as your great-grandfather used to say, 'started fiddling around with how folks did and didn't do things.' Naturally, since he was a minister, he was horrified that Fours Crossing didn't have a church — folks used to worship in each other's houses, I guess. Well, as you know from your own daddy, Melissa, us New Englanders can be mighty stubborn; since the folks in Fours Crossing had never had a minister or a church, they didn't see that they needed one just because some busybody from Massachusetts said they did. Bradford Ellison started out being what today people would politely call a 'controversial figure.' Back then, though, I guess people just plain disliked him — no offense, Jed."

Jed smiled absentmindedly at Gran. Melissa passed Gran another doughnut and started to pass the plate to Jed, too, but the look on his face stopped her. Maybe it was the flickering light, but his eyes were puzzled, as if he had heard something in Gran's story that wasn't right there in its words. Maybe, she thought, he's trying to figure out more about why Bradford Ellison was controversial. But somehow it seemed like a lot more than that.

"Well," said Gran, refusing a second doughnut, "it seems that Bradford Ellison had some pretty learned people down in Boston writing things for him to say to the folks up here to bring them around to his way of thinking. And sure enough, after a while some began to think that a church might be nice after all — and then after a longer while pretty much everyone else came around — everyone except old Eli. Around that time, too, Eli's only son,

Eben, up and fell in love with Bradford Ellison's daughter Tabitha, and that just about finished Eli. He was so mad and bitter and sad that he just packed up and went out to the woods to where the family sawmill was, on some land that was owned by the whole village in common — " Gran turned to Melissa again. "I should explain, Melissa," she said, "that there were so few people in Fours Crossing in those days that most everyone, no matter how important, did some kind of laboring work, and what the Dunns did was supply the village with firewood and lumber. Well, as I was saying, old Eli went out to the sawmill and he built the house you saw today, and moved in. All he took with him, supposedly, was an old oak chest that he wouldn't let anyone look into. Young Eben stayed in Fours Crossing and married Tabitha Ellison, and eventually they moved into this very house and raised a passel of sons and daughters. No one could ever talk old Eli into coming back, though the story goes that Eben and Tabitha tried over and over again to mend the rift between their two families. It never was healed till after old Eli died — or whatever; no one ever knew quite what finally happened to him out there in the woods — some kind of accident, people thought, at least so your great-grandfather used to say. Anyway, whatever the reason, old Eli dropped plumb out of sight a year or two after his son married. After he was gone, the Dunns and the Ellisons got to be friends again, and most of the Dunns from then on were good solid citizens and churchgoers — till they started leaving the village, that is, which a lot of them eventually did — like your daddy,

Melissa. I guess Fours Crossing is just too small for some folks."

"Wasn't there some kind of apology, sort of?" Jed asked.

"Yes." Gran nodded. "To try to heal the rift. A while after Eben's marriage, the town of Fours Crossing gave one acre of the common land around the sawmill to the Dunn family forever — that made Eli the legal owner of the land he'd put his house on. The town also decided to let the job of Forest Keeper — supplying the town with wood and with the Festival tree — stay in the Dunn family forever. It has, too. Today, of course, most people cut or buy their own wood. And the old sawmill fell to pieces years ago. But the Keeper still provides the Festival tree; that hasn't changed since old Eli's day."

"Is the hermit the Forest Keeper now?" Melissa asked.

"Yes," Gran told her. "He's from the branch of the family that goes most directly back to old Eli. But the hermit's the first Dunn for generations who's taken being Keeper seriously enough to actually live out there. You'd think he'd keep the old house up more, since he's made it his home, but I don't think he's even tried. In fact, every Spring Festival, when we go out to get the tree, I half expect to see that the poor old place has blown down during the winter!"

"How come the tree has to come from there?" Melissa asked curiously. "I mean, why go all the way out into the woods for a tree when there are hundreds all over the place?"

"I don't think anyone knows that," said Jed softly. "Do they?"

"If they do" — Gran smiled — "they're not telling. It's like many old customs, I guess. Its origins are lost so far back in time no one really remembers how the custom itself began or where it came from."

Gran paused a moment, looking into the lamp flame, as if to make sure it really was steady now — but she's not even seeing it, Melissa thought; she's almost as far away as Jed was before.

"Odd," said Gran at last, rousing herself, "how things change. But I daresay folks just can't be bothered. For instance, now at Festival time the villagers go only as far as the Keeper's House — the hermit's — and stay there — though it's true the Selectmen go into the woods with the hermit to get the tree. But when your great-grandfather was a boy, Melissa, *his* great-grandfather told him that in the old days the whole village went far into the woods to a place where there was an old cave — a root cellar, your great-grandfather said he was told it was — a place where people stored vegetables before there was refrigeration. He said the Indians probably built it, or maybe old Eli — no one really quite knew. And no one knows now just where it was, but every Festival in the old days, that's where they'd all go and . . . Goodness!" Gran suddenly jumped up, interrupting herself. "Talking about Festival so much reminds me — and I'd better do it now before I forget again!" She went across the room and pulled open a drawer.

"Do what?" Melisa asked, mystified, sorry the story seemed over.

Gran held up a hammer. "Call it vanity" — she laughed — "but I've been thinking I'd like to re-arrange those plates a bit before Festival, so they won't look so much as if one's missing. And now that we know the fourth one's not coming back — well, they needn't look forlorn any more, it seems to me, with that empty space. Besides, Festival's a happy time." Gran went into the dining room and called, "Just bring the lamp, children, would you, please?"

Jed and Melissa followed, Jed with the lamp. Melissa shivered; the closed-up room was chilly and damp. The kerosene flame threw shadows eerily against the whitewashed wall as Gran rehung the three silver plates in a straight horizontal line, par-tially hiding the fourth plate's pale empty space.

"There," she said cheerfully, stepping back to survey what she'd done. "That'll look better, don't you think, when people look in through the window on Spring Festival?" She rubbed her hands briskly together as if to warm them. "Now, who's for a pic-ture puzzle? There's one with a nice winter scene, perfect for tonight — I'll just get it out of the cup-board. Melissa, you might stir up the fire . . . Well, come along, children, out of the cold, for heaven's sake!"

"It looks funny, Miz Dunn," Jed muttered, still holding the lamp by the dining-room door; the three plates gleamed warmly in its flickering light. "They formed a circle before, four round plates in a round circle — it was nice. Now they're — they're nothing, all in a row like that."

"Maybe, but now it's harder to tell there's one missing," Gran said over her shoulder. "And before you know it, we'll all forget there ever were four, and the poor old hermit will have one pretty thing, at least, to brighten his drab life. Come on back now, Jed, and shut the door. Let's keep the heat in."

That night, for the first time in more than a month, Melissa had no dreams about her mother. Instead, she kept seeing the silvery fourth plate shining faintly from far away in the woods, like a lonely, distant star. And once, waking when the wind rattled her windows and seemed to shake the whole house, she thought she heard the dog Ulfin howling mournfully under her window.

6

It was a little like having a brother, waking up the next morning and knowing Jed was in the house. And it had been like having a whole family again the night before, sitting cozily around the table with him and with Gran. What a tale that was, about old Eli Dunn! Melissa had never dreamed that her own family went back so far or had such a complicated history.

Melissa rolled over and reached for her bedside lamp. Maybe if the power was still off there'd be no school and the wonderful cozy feeling could go on all day.

But the lamp went on, and Gran called, "Melissa — breakfast!" from downstairs.

The kitchen was warm with the now-familiar smells of oatmeal and cocoa. When Melissa went in, Jed was staring down into his full oatmeal bowl as if trying to decide whether to use a spoon or a fork.

"What's the matter, Jethro?" Gran asked, twinkling. "Don't you like oatmeal? Here — put some more milk on it. Like as not there'll be no more deliveries again for a while after the storm last night. Might as well use the last of the old milk before it turns. Eat up, boy; it's good Scottish porridge! I'm surprised at you!"

"My people aren't Scottish, I guess, Miz Dunn."

"Would you rather have bread and jam?"

"Yes'm," Jed answered meekly.

Melissa tried not to be envious as Gran cut two slices of her wonderful bread and spread them with butter and jam for Jed. It wasn't that she didn't like Gran's oatmeal; it was just that there were other things she liked more. Bacon and eggs, for instance . . .

There was a sudden banging at the back door and they all three jumped up. Pride and Joy, mewing, left his place by the hearth and sprang onto the table.

"Gracious!" said Gran. "I wonder who that can be." She wiped her hands on her apron and went to the door, then stepped back, saying, "Well, Seth Ellison, you certainly did give us a turn."

"Dad!" said Jed, stepping quickly in front of him, as if to hide him from Melissa.

" 'Mornin', all," said Mr. Ellison, slurring his words together. " 'Squite a storm last night — nothin' like havin' to spend it all alone," he said, glaring at Jed, whose face was bright red with embarrassment.

Melissa was unable to take her eyes off Mr. Ellison's many layers of soiled work clothes and the several days' growth of beard that made his face look dirty.

"Lef' me las' night, didn't you, lad?" said Mr. Ellison, swaying a little as he loomed threateningly over his son.

"Now, Seth," said Gran firmly, "we phoned you up and told you there was no point in Jed's going back down the hill in a blizzard, long as you were all right, which you seemed to be."

Seth Ellison raised his hand and hit Jed clumsily across the face.

For a minute none of them moved.

"Don't think you had any call to do that," Gran said softly, but still not moving. "The boy had been out getting wood for me, and it was my doing he didn't go home. I told you on the phone . . ."

"You're not staying out any more nights, lad, you hear? Or you'll get a lot more'n that. As for you, Miz Dunn, I'll thank you to keep your interfering eyes and ears away from my fam'ly, and your clutches off my boy. As I've said before." He swayed again, glancing toward Melissa. "Dunno who you are, girl," he said rudely, "but if you're the reason my boy was out all night this time, I'll . . ."

"That will do, Seth," Gran snapped. She grabbed her heavy lumberjacket off a hook and pushed him outside, slamming the door behind them both. Melissa could hear their voices but not what they were saying.

Jed went to the sink and got himself a glass of water.

"It — it's okay, Jed," Melissa said, wanting desperately to make him feel better.

"It's not okay," he said bitterly. "He gets worse all the time. I — I hate him."

Jed's face closed quickly, as if he felt he'd said too much, and Melissa remembered what Gran had said about his not talking much until his troubles boiled over. But before she could think of what to say to encourage him to talk more, he started for the back door. Then he seemed to realize his father was still there and bolted into the dining room instead.

Melissa let him go, still wondering what she could possibly say to him. No wonder he was moody sometimes! It was worse, far worse, than anything she'd imagined.

She was just about to start washing the dishes when Jed called to her in an oddly choked voice, and heart pounding though she didn't know why, she ran to him.

He was standing in front of one long wall, staring down at the floor.

The three silver plates were lying at his feet — forming a neat circle, with space left for the fourth, just as they had on the wall before Gran had rearranged them.

"Holy cow," breathed Jed. "That can't have been an accident."

Melissa stared down at the floor, too, not believing what she saw. Then she understood, and laughed in relief. "The wind," she said, "the wind must've blown them down. Didn't you hear it last night?"

"No." Jed's eyes were still on the plates and his voice was very soft.

"No! But it must have been, Jed, what else . . .?"

"I don't know," he said strangely. "But it wasn't the wind. How could it have been? How could the wind blow the plates back into their old pattern?"

"Well, I — oh, I don't know," sputtered Melissa. "Coincidence, I guess. It can't have been anything else."

"It wasn't the wind," he said with conviction. "And it wasn't coincidence. It's a sign — a sign that something terrible's going on here!"

Jed bolted from the room before Melissa could speak, grabbed his jacket, his boots, and his snowshoes from the kitchen, and ran out the back door.

He kept himself aloof all day. At lunch he sat alone, and during the brief Spring Festival rehearsal after school, he wouldn't even look at Melissa, or so it seemed to her. As she marched across the gym with the other seventh-graders, she tried to get his attention, but his face remained closed to her; she couldn't decide if he was just preoccupied or if she had done something unforgivable.

But what? What could she possibly have done?

Was it so wrong to point out that it had to have been the wind that blew the plates down?

When everyone sang the Festival song, Melissa had to look down at the words that the music teacher had written out for her, but nevertheless she tried to sing extra loud as she passed Jed.

He still didn't look at her. Not once during rehearsal did he even acknowledge she was there.

Okay, she tried to tell herself as she snowshoed home alone, that's how he is; you can't make him talk to you any more than you can make the postcard Daddy sent into a letter.

No more than Gran can make you talk about Mum, either, Melissa, something inside her said — but she ignored it.

Jed was at Gran's ahead of her; she could just see the top of his head over the drifts near the henhouse. She started to go into the house, but Gran lifted up a feed bucket and beckoned, so she joined them reluctantly, not quite knowing how to act toward Jed.

But it didn't matter. He didn't even seem to notice she was there.

"Let's see," Gran was saying as Melissa came up. "June, I think — yes, it must have been June when the plate was taken, around the fifth." She smiled, scattering feed on the snow for the hungrily scratching chickens. "Goodness, how could I forget? It got so terribly hot that week — remember, Jed?" She handed a bucket to Melissa and motioned to her to put some feed outside the chickens' pen for the wild birds. "Seems to me last summer was as early as this spring is late."

Jed's eyes widened then. "Miz Dunn," he said excitedly, "you remember last Spring Festival? Remember how the hermit seemed madder than usual when we came to get the tree — and how he yelled, 'You'll see — I'll get you yet!' or something like that when we left?"

Gran smiled again. " 'I'll get you *all*!' " she said. "Yes, I remember. We all wondered what imagined hurt that poor old soul had stored up in his mind against us."

Jed turned abruptly away and ran toward the house.

Gran shook her head, watching him. "Now I wonder what's got into Jed," she said. "Do you know, Melissa?"

"He's hardly spoken to me all day." Furiously, Melissa threw the last handful of feed onto the ground. "And if he's going to go on being like that, I don't even care if he ever does!"

Gran gave her a long look and then took a hammer down from a shelf just inside the henhouse door. She handed it to Melissa with a box of roofing nails. "Best thing I know for a good mad is hammering," she said. "If the henhouse roof doesn't get pounded down before dark, it's sure to snow again tonight and then I'll have to shovel it off again before I can fix it. Here — I'll give you a boost up."

7

For the next few days, although he did manage to mutter "Good morning" occasionally, Jed continued to be drawn as close inside himself as a snail is in its shell. He didn't even seem to notice Tommy enough to growl at him for following him around. Each afternoon, without waiting for Melissa, Jed strapped on his snowshoes and set off by himself. One afternoon, he did go to Gran's, but he barricaded himself in the dining room, shutting Melissa out.

"Just leave him be, lambie," Gran advised — but even she seemed worried. "If I know him, he's figuring something out, and he won't tell anyone anything till he's good and ready. He probably doesn't even know he's being — well, the way he's being."

Melissa tried not to mind; she too could see there was something troubling Jed badly. But it was lonely without him, and even though Tommy Coffin seemed more friendly than ever, Tommy wasn't anywhere near the same. Then, to make things worse, Melissa got another short postcard from her father. All it said was:

Dear Pigeon,
    In Montana now, very cold. Lots of clients seen this trip. Miss you. Have fun.

Love,
Daddy

Have fun! Sure.

On the night before Spring Festival, Gran poured the last of the milk into a pot for cocoa and said with less than her usual cheerfulness, "We'll have to do with powdered for a while, I guess. They say down at the store that no milk'll get in for the next few days — there was a snowslide up at Hiltonville. And that means the Fours Crossing farmers who have cows won't be able to take their milk to be pasteurized. Can't have you drinking raw milk, can we?" Gran set the powdered milk box down on the table and took out a big pitcher to mix it in.

"I guess not," said Melissa. She read the ingredients on the box and made a face. "It's depressing, isn't it, Gran?"

"What is, lambie?"

"Running out of things. Having snow all the time. Sometimes I think if I have to shovel any more, I'll — I don't know. Spit, I guess, or break the shovel."

Gran sat down at the kitchen table opposite her. "And Jed's not making it any easier, is he? I know — it's what I worried might happen. And now it has. Melissa, if you want to go back to Boston, I can always write your daddy."

"I don't want to go back to Boston! And besides, I bet Daddy wouldn't come home anyway. All he ever sends is those dumb postcards, and they don't even say anything . . ."

"They say 'love' at the end," Gran said gently. "He means that, you know."

"I guess."

Gran reached out and patted her hand. "Well, tree cutting's before the birds are up tomorrow morning," she said, "and Festival's right after. That should cheer us both. Now let's hustle up and make supper so we can get a few hours' sleep before the tree cutting."

The beginning of dawn threw the trees into high relief against the sky when Melissa went sleepily with Gran and the other villagers into the forest. Even Tommy, his eyes on Jed up with the Eights, seemed awed into silence as soon as they crossed into the woods on the other side of the wall. The trees made a myriad of tangled shadows on the ground, the snow blue-white and silver between them. It was soon bright enough for the villagers to blow out the kerosene lanterns they had brought, and to switch off their flashlights. The branches were soft with a new powdery dusting of snow, but the forest was still and cold, brittle and mysterious, early on this day that would be as long as its night.

The villagers moved through the woods like a band of medieval travelers, muffled in thick coats and warm scarves, most of which were still muted to black or gray in the dim cold light. The eighth-graders were up ahead in a group, but almost all the other people were with their families; no one talked except in whispers. But then, as the light grew:

" 'Here we come a-wassailing,' " someone sang with sudden merriness as the group emerged from the first stand of hemlocks and went into the bare deciduous forest.

" 'Among the leaves so green,' " boomed the Chairman of the Board of Selectmen, another Mr. Ellison, Henry this time, and as usual no immediate relation to Jed. Someone pointed up at the bare branches, and there was laughter. Soon the whole crowd was singing. It warmed her, Melissa found, just when she was beginning to be uncomfortably conscious of the cold.

A new voice started the song up again just as it ended: "Come a-schwash-a-sching," it sang drunkenly. Melissa turned around to see Jed's father reeling up the path toward the group under the trees. He wore only his indoor clothes plus a thin coat and scarf — no hat, no gloves. "He's got his drink to keep him warm," someone muttered. "Doesn't need any wassail, that one! Probably been at it all night." Then Melissa saw Jed burst away from the other eighth-graders and run into the forest.

For a moment she stood uncertainly next to Tommy, watching.

"Oh, Christmas," said Tommy fiercely. "Christmas — everyone saw! And — hey, Melissa!"

By then Melissa had made her decision and was running through the woods after Jed.

"Come on back, lad!" she heard Seth Ellison shout, and then add pathetically, "You don' wanna 'sociate with the likes of me — I know. Go on, then — run off, I don' know's I care!"

Melissa went on running, following Jed's tracks.

He wasn't hard to find, slumped against a birch tree near a snowy hump that would probably be revealed as a boulder if spring ever came.

He had his back to her, and she realized as soon as she reached him that she didn't know what to do.

"Jed?" she asked timidly. "You — you want me to go away?"

Jed shook his head. Melissa could see that his fists were round balls, tightly clenched in their double layer of mittens. "He always spoils everything," he said thickly. "Every time I want to do anything, he busts it all up. It's special, being in the eighth grade at Festival time. We — have special things to do — you'll see. It's wrong to hate your father. I don't want to. But I can't help it. Sometimes I wish — I wish he were dead, too!"

"Too?" she asked, forgetting.

"You're not the only one without a mother."

From very far away, Melissa heard the "Wassail Song" start up again. Mum had liked that song . . .

But there was Jed, hunched against the tree.

And there she was, hunched inside herself and her own memories, unable to find words to say to comfort a friend, even though she'd wanted him to talk and now he'd finally started.

"Melissa," he said suddenly. "Look."

In the shadows watching them, feathery tail waving gently, was the dog Ulfin. He watched them for a moment longer, then whined and pawed impatiently at the snow.

"What does he want?" Melissa whispered. The shift in focus made words easier to find. "Jed, what's going on? Why won't you tell me anything? What did you mean before when you said the plates were a sign and that something terrible is going on?"

"I — I wish I knew," he said. "I don't understand, but . . . Melissa, it keeps sticking in my mind that those plates aren't plates at all, but — but something else."

"Gran said herself she wasn't sure."

"But if they're not plates," said Jed, "what are they? And how come they put themselves back in order? How come this dog keeps — pestering me, making me do what he wants, making me think he wants you to do it, too? Maybe I'm crazy, I can't begin to explain it. But I — I keep thinking, the hermit cursed everyone at Festival last year, I mean really cursed, like a threat. Then in a couple of months your gran's plate — or whatever — was stolen, and the hermit's got it now. And this darned dog . . ."

Ulfin whined again and leaped up and down in the snow, making little half turns toward the hermit's clearing, begging them to follow.

Melissa watched him, remembering how his tracks had disappeared and then appeared again in the snow.

"All I can think," Jed went on, "is that we have to get the fourth plate back. Or someone does, but it looks like me, or us — us probably; the dog always comes when you're around. Maybe if we got the plate back, we'd understand. Maybe we should just take it at tree cutting, if there's a chance. Maybe we ..."

He stopped, then rubbed his forehead as if trying to clear his mind. "I do keep saying 'we,' don't I? But that's not fair. I've been trying to keep you out of it. It's not your town ..."

"It's my gran's plate," Melissa said quickly.

She went closer to Ulfin, who stopped leaping and nuzzled her hand as if to encourage her.

Her words came out before she was aware of thinking them. "I'll help if you want, Jed, with whatever it is."

"Are you sure?"

"Yes." But she felt partly as if something outside herself had made her say it.

Jed gave her a searching look and then quietly said, "Good." He patted Ulfin, then said, "I've got to go back to the Eights," as if telling the dog as much as Melissa. "But I'll see you later, when we all get to the clearing. Okay?"

"Okay."

When she turned to watch Jed go back to his classmates, Melissa saw Tommy leaning against a tree, watching them silently from just out of earshot. She turned back again in confusion and realized Ulfin was gone. Again there were no tracks, and she stared down at the snow, trying to sort out what had just happened. It was as if there were suddenly two worlds in the forest — Tommy from one and Ulfin from the other, with her and Jed in between.

And yet that couldn't be.

She went back to Tommy.

"Is Jed okay?" he asked as soon as she was close enough to hear.

She nodded, startled at the misery in his eyes.

"I — I'd have come and helped," he said, looking at his snowshoes, "but — well, he sometimes doesn't want me around when . . . I guess Jed really likes you, huh?"

By then Melissa had sifted through her thoughts enough to realize that Tommy was really hurt and that of course he would want to be the one Jed turned to when he was in trouble.

"I — I guess," she said uncomfortably. "I like him, anyway."

Tommy knelt in the snow and seemed to be adjusting his snowshoe binding. But the binding looked fine to Melissa.

"I'm sorry if I butted in," she said softly. "You've known him for longer. But — well, I didn't think about that; maybe I'd have waited if I had. It — it must be awful to have a father like that."

"It *is*," Tommy said emphatically.

"Does Mr. Ellison get that way a lot?"

Tommy nodded. Then the words poured out quickly as if his knowledge of the situation could somehow restore him to a position of importance in Jed's eyes as well as in Melissa's. "He's not so bad when he'd sober — really, he's not. And I think he likes Jed underneath, but he can't show it. He — he's been drinking more lately, though. They live in this real little house, next door to us, you know? And it's Jed who has to do everything — cook and clean and stuff. But he never says anything about it. He never says anything bad about his father."

Melissa winced, thinking of what Jed had said to her. But she certainly wasn't going to hurt Tommy more by telling him that.

Tommy's voice dropped and he turned away again. "It — sometimes it's like he's a — some kind of loyal knight or something. You know — bound by a vow so he can't complain or go away or anything." Tommy suddenly pulled at his cap, as if trying to hide embarrassment.

"And his father doesn't deserve him, right?" Melissa asked gently.

"Well — sometimes he doesn't." Tommy's face was red as his hair when he faced her again. "I can't believe I said that." He shook his head, grinning sheepishly.

"It's okay," she said. "I won't tell Jed."

Tommy smiled gratefully. Then, as they moved back to where the villagers' tracks made a clear path in the gradually brightening light, Tommy tugged her arm suddenly and said, "You know what? I bet we could cut around ahead of the others, so you'll be right up front when we get to the hermit's. Want to?"

"Sure," said Melissa, glad to agree.

Tommy hurried her back into the woods, parallel to the villagers' trail, but then straight as their tracks curved. "The hermit yells these great curses," he explained enthusiastically on the way, as if nothing out of the ordinary had happened. "Like out of an old book or something. Last year he yelled, 'Begone from the forest of winter!' at everyone and, 'May icicles impale your hearts forever!' and, 'May cold and endless winter freeze your blood!' — it's great. Melissa — did you hear me?"

"Yes," said Melissa, shaking herself back to attention. But the sinister sound of *May cold and endless winter freeze your blood!* echoed in her mind until they reached the hermit's clearing and Tommy stopped, pointing.

And there was the hermit again — Eli John Dunn, her relative — a silent and this time oddly dignified figure. As Melissa and Tommy watched, he lifted his arms slowly to the pale sky, making his voluminous black sleeves flow down, exposing his gnarled hands and bony wrists.

"He must be cold," whispered Tommy. "He looks as if he's praying or something."

He did look that way, although no sound came from his lips and he hardly seemed to breathe once his arms were raised. Melissa felt a sudden pang of sympathy for him — he seemed so totally alone, and somehow she couldn't believe he didn't mind. Flakes of snow drifted down to his beard and eyebrows and perched for a moment on the bushy hairs before melting, but still the old man did not move.

There was no sign of the silver plate, though the

tripod was still there — and then Melissa realized just how hard Jed's plan was going to be to carry out. It would be one thing to snatch the plate and run, but quite another to have to hunt for it.

Out of the corner of her eye, Melissa saw something move on the other side of the path, and then Jed came out from the woods and squatted down behind a tree for cover, watching the hermit, too.

"There's Jed," she whispered. "I'm going over."

"Me, too," said Tommy. "But keep down. The hermit'll see."

They scrunched down low, and crossed the path.

But even so, the hermit looked right at them, and sympathy or no sympathy, Melissa shuddered as he extended his arm toward her, still in absolute silence, all five claw-like fingers outstretched and pointing. Melissa looked only long enough to see his cold black eyes bore into hers. Then she felt something push against her legs, between her and the hermit. Luckily she saw it was Ulfin in time to stop herself from screaming. Tommy didn't seem to notice.

Ulfin pushed again, and she realized he wanted her to go closer to Jed, out of the hermit's line of vision. As soon as she understood, Ulfin faded back into the woods.

"The hermit saw you," Jed reproached them. He glared at Tommy. "I should think you'd have known to keep behind stuff as well as down."

"I'm sorry, Jed," Tommy said humbly. But he looked pleased that Jed had at least spoken to him.

Melissa squatted down next to Jed as Tommy got on his other side.

"We'd better wait," Jed said to her, "till the others get here and start bargaining for the tree. No one'll notice if we start looking then." He glanced at Tommy, his annoyance seeming to grow. "Aren't you supposed to be with the Sevens?"

"Oh, come on, Jed," Melissa said quickly. "I'm not with the Sevens, either."

"But we've got work to do," Jed whispered to her. "We — right?"

"Right," she answered firmly, as much to herself as to him. "But . . ."

There was a shout down the path, and the villagers began to arrive. They were marching in an orderly procession with Mr. Henry Ellison, as Chairman of the Board of Selectmen, in the lead. As Henry Ellison moved forward, the tall, black-robed hermit slowly turned and dropped his arms. Melissa heard Jed gasp as the old man's hands fell away from his face.

"He's smiling!" Jed whispered loudly. "No one's ever seen him smile. It's almost a legend how stern he always looks and how angry he is when we come to cut the tree. But that's a real smile!"

"Darn it," said Tommy. "I bet he's not even going to curse."

"Something's very wrong," Jed muttered. "It's not going right. It's not supposed to be like this."

Smiling benignly while the villagers, who were obviously as confused as Jed, whispered and stared, the hermit walked toward Mr. Ellison. Mr. Ellison, also looking bewildered, walked slowly to meet him. When they were a few paces apart, the hermit bowed and extended his hand.

"Welcome to the forest of winter, Henry Ellison," said the hermit in a reedy voice that nonetheless had great strength in it. He bowed again. "You have come for the tree?"

Mr. Ellison nodded, apparently speechless.

"He never says that," whispered Jed. "Not this hermit — though I've heard in the old days the Keeper was always nice about the tree. But I've never heard it done like this!"

"Right," Tommy whispered eagerly to Melissa. "This is where he's supposed to start yelling. Hey — I remember another one he said last year: 'Traitors, begone from this sacred wood!' — remember, Jed? That was pretty good, but I still like the icicles one best, that and 'May cold and endless . . .' "

"Shut *up*!" Jed whispered fiercely. He prodded Melissa. "In just a minute now," he began — then: "Look — he's taking Mr. Ellison off to look for a tree; the others are starting to follow . . ."

"Usually," Tommy went on, avoiding Jed's eyes, "the hermit tries to stop the chairman first and tells him he'll chop *him* down if he takes a tree. And then — well, at least that's what's happened each time I've come," he finished when Jed wheeled on him. "Maybe it doesn't always, huh?"

"Tommy," said Melissa as gently as she could, "Jed and I have something to do, and . . ."

Jed held up his hand.

The dog Ulfin came out of the woods again and this time went directly to Tommy, wagging his tail in such a real-dog way Melissa had to look twice to be sure it was he.

"Whose dog?" asked Tommy. "Hey — look. He

77

must want me to follow him." He smiled and patted Ulfin's head. "Good dog. Do you think I should go with him?"

"Yes," said Jed. "Yes, yes, yes!"

"Well, okay," Tommy said dubiously. Ulfin gently nudged him toward an out-of-the-way clump of trees. "Whose dog is he anyway?"

"We don't . . ." began Melissa.

"Mine," Jed interrupted.

Tommy looked at Jed in astonishment.

"Well, he's sort of wild," Jed said hastily. "But he's sort of mine, too."

"What's his name?" Tommy asked skeptically.

"Ulfin. Go on, Tommy, he must have something to show you."

"You'd think it'd be you he'd want," said Tommy to Jed, hesitating.

Ulfin nudged him again, harder this time.

"Go on, Tom," urged Jed. "We'll come soon. He won't let you get lost." Melissa could see that Jed's eyes were following the hermit and Mr. Ellison as they moved deeper into the forest. They were now quite far from the hermit's house — and then suddenly they both turned their backs to it.

Immediately Ulfin put his front paws in the middle of Tommy's chest, knocking him down and covering his face with huge, un-Ulfin-like licks — to distract him, Melissa felt sure. Jed grabbed Melissa's hand and they both raced to the house. The hermit and Mr. Ellison still had their backs turned and the villagers, Melissa fervently hoped as she ran, were paying careful attention to the tree transaction —

Mr. Ellison, she saw, was calling to one of the men in the crowd to bring a saw.

Then there was the creak of rusty hinges and a sharp push from Jed. A musty smell hit Melissa's nostrils, and then they were inside the hermit's house.

8

The hermit's house was worse than musty. It
was a dark, sparsely furnished, rickety shell
that smelled of mice, as if it had never been
cleaned or aired in the forty years the hermit had
lived there. The small high windows, Melissa saw,
had no glass — just the loosely fastened shutters
she'd seen from the outside — and on the inside, the
windows were curtained only with cobwebs. The
bare floor was made of wide, deeply scarred boards;
the walls were rough unfinished plaster; and the low
ceiling was striped with thick dark beams, from which
more cobwebs hung.

The first thing Melissa and Jed both saw was the
steep, narrow staircase directly opposite the door;
the next, the fireplace in the small room to their
left. A feeble fire smoldered there, adding its dim
glow to the thin light that trickled uncertainly in

through the cracks in the shutters. Suspended over
the fireplace on a heavy crane like Gran's was a
large black pot. (Witch's caldron, thought Melissa
with trepidation as she peered carefully into it — but
it was empty.)

A straw broom leaned against the fireplace frame
and a pair of old andirons rose dimly over the ashes,
but there was no mantelpiece. A few basic cooking
utensils — a couple of pewter spoons, a skillet,
another pot — hung from a nearby beam. Rocks of
various shapes and colors, some quite beautiful, were
arranged with surprising care on a shelf above the
table; old quill pens made a feathery bouquet in an
incongruously modern tin can hanging from the wall
beneath it.

Melissa was just examining the rocks when Jed
came in from the other room, the one to the right
of the door. "There's nothing much in there," he
said, but Melissa went in anyway.

The room Jed had come from was bare except for
a fireplace that backed up on the one she'd just
left — and the outline of what looked like a tall, narrow cupboard door next to the fireplace. There was
no doorknob, so Melissa ran her finger gently around
the door's outline, feeling for some way to open it.
Almost by accident her hand touched what looked
like an ordinary knot in the wood — and the door
sprung open, revealing a dark closet-like room with
rough wooden walls and a floor so carpeted with
acorn shells it looked as if squirrels lived there. The
smell was musty enough to make Melissa want to
hold her breath.

"Jed," she called, turning away from the smell. "Jed!"

She tried to ignore the mustiness enough to go back in, first propping the door open with a log from the fireplace. Almost immediately, her knee struck something low and hard — some kind of box, maybe?

"What's the matter?" Jed asked, coming up behind her. "You sounded as if you'd seen — holy cow!"

"Do you still have those matches?" she asked without turning around.

"Yes," he said, "and I saw a couple of candles in the other room."

When he came back and held a lighted candle in the doorway, they both gasped. There at the back of the tiny room was a large oak chest, softly gleaming as if it had just been polished — or at least opened frequently; there was no dust on it, Melissa noticed.

Jed whistled softly and knelt beside Melissa in front of the chest. " 'All he took with him,' " he said softly — and Melissa nodded, knowing instantly that he was quoting Gran's story about the first Eli Dunn — " 'was an old oak chest . . .' "

"Could it really be the same one?" Melissa whispered, in awe of it. "So long ago — hundreds of years?"

"Sure. Wood lasts. Look at houses, furniture . . ."

" 'An old oak chest,' " said Melissa, " 'that he wouldn't let anyone look into.' "

"Well, *we're* going to look into it," Jed announced

decisively, putting both hands on the heavy, gracefully rounded lid.

It was surprisingly easy to open; it lifted as silently and smoothly as if it had been oiled the day before, without a creak or a groan — as if someone had been lifting it often, over and over again, down through the centuries — except, thought Melissa, surely that would have worn out the hinges?

"Holy cow," exclaimed Jed again, peering into the chest. "Look — look at all this stuff!"

Melissa leaned over his shoulder, then reached at the same time he did for the soft white garment that lay, neatly folded, on top of what seemed to be a large pile of odds and ends. The garment looked a little like the choir robes in church back in Boston, Melissa thought. But then, when Jed held it up to the light that came from the main room, she realized it wasn't like them at all; its fabric was far softer — a smooth, finely spun, loosely woven wool. Its cut was perfectly plain and it was unornamented except for a thin gold belt that slipped through two small holes in the sides.

"Whew," whistled Jed, fingering the gold. "Remind you of anything?"

It hit Melissa then that the cut of this robe was like the hermit's black one — and that the three slender braided gold strands exactly matched Ulfin's collar — as if one had been made from the other.

"And look," Jed went on, pointing, "there's another one — only it's all yellow and cobwebby." He lifted up what looked like an ancestor of the white robe — woolen, but so dried out with age it was more like brittle gauze than wool. The worn shoulders of the old robe cracked dustily and the robe fell away from Jed's hands, tumbling into a fragile-looking heap on the floor.

"Rats!" said Jed, looking embarrassed.

Melissa tried to scoop the material up without damaging it further. "Oh, Jed, what if he finds out?" she said.

But Jed was examining the newer robe again. "I bet this one's a copy," he said excitedly. "A copy of the old one. Yes, I'm sure it is! But why . . .?"

Melissa looked again, comparing the decaying garment in her hands to the freshly gleaming one Jed was holding up. "You're right," she said finally, as she gently laid what was left of the antique robe back in its corner of the chest. "Only I can't answer why, either."

Jed burrowed into another corner of the chest. "There's a queer sort of dagger here," he said, "and a couple of sort of cup things and — wow, Melissa, look at all these old books!"

The villagers' voices came close to the door, making them both freeze, but then the voices faded, passing by.

"They've picked the tree now, I think," Jed whispered. "We'd better leave."

Melissa nodded abstractedly, barely hearing him. She had picked up the smallest of the books and was holding it binding up, fingering some odd, foreign-looking letters on its spine. The hermit a scholar? It didn't seem likely. "Jed," she said, "look at this a minute."

"We've got to hurry, Melissa," he said, sounding annoyed — but as soon as he'd looked over her shoulder at what she was holding, he whistled, low and surprised. "Holy cow," he said. "It's — holy, holy cow!"

"Are you thinking what I'm thinking?" asked Melissa.

"If you're thinking that the writing on that book looks like the squiggles on your gran's silver plates, yes, then I am."

"That *is* what I'm thinking," said Melissa. "And if the squiggles *are* letters, or stand for letters . . . That's it!" she said excitedly. "Instead of being a foreign kind of writing, it could be a secret kind — a cipher, a sort of code . . ."

"It's not a real book," said Jed, examining it. "It's like those blank ones people buy to keep diaries in, except it looks awfully old."

Melissa took the book back from him. The crumbling reddish-brown binding did seem more curved than a real printed book's would have been. She felt one of the pages carefully between two fingers. It was brittle, a bit like onionskin paper; it crackled as if age had dried it, and it had a brownish-yellow tinge. The letters, or whatever they were, though neat, were spidery thin and had obviously been painstakingly written by hand, not printed. Her excitement grew; she'd thought of cipher because her math teacher had given her class some ciphers to solve last year for extra credit and had spent a couple of periods explaining how it was done — Melissa had been fascinated. Somehow the idea of this book's being in cipher didn't seem farfetched at all now that she was sure Jed was right about it's not being printed. And if the squiggles really were like the ones on Gran's plates . . .

There was a sudden burst of laughter from outside, and then applause.

Melissa opened the book again quickly and peered at the squiggles on the first page. "I bet it *is* written in cipher," she began, "because — " But Jed grabbed her arm. "We'd better go," he said. "I don't think the hermit's going to be very friendly if he catches us here." He tugged urgently at the book even though Melissa had the first few pages between her thumb and forefinger. The binding gently gave way and Melissa found herself still holding the pages, while Jed, apparently not noticing, tossed the rest of the book back into the chest, slammed the door shut — tighter this time; its outline barely showed — and ran out of the room. "Come on!" he called urgently. "We'll have to look for the plate another time. Come on!"

But Melissa stooped first to pick up another page that had fallen to the floor. She slipped it with the other ones inside her jacket before she hurried after Jed.

They were just in time. The sun, a pink-gold ball, was hanging low in the sky behind the house, lending its chilly glow to the snow on nearby branches. The villagers were preparing to go home; Mr. Henry Ellison had leaned a small, perfectly shaped pine tree against his shoulder and was balancing it there carefully as the sun made rainbow jewels of the moisture on its branches. Mr. Ellison said one last

86

thing to the hermit, who luckily was standing with his back to the house as Jed and Melissa, two dark shadows against the rapidly brightening snow, darted out and around the edge of the clearing to rejoin the villagers.

"Where are those stout eighth-grade lads," Mr. Ellison boomed, "who are going to take our tree back for us?"

Jed, with a quick warning glance at Melissa that said *Don't tell anyone where we've been*, seized one of his classmates by the shoulder and pushed through the crowd. "Here we are, Mr. Ellison," he said, as if he'd been eagerly waiting for that moment all along.

"Good enough." Mr. Ellison steadied the tree carefully as Jed and his classmate lifted it. The other boy led, Jed followed, and the procession of villagers slowly wound its way back through the forest, away from the hermit's house.

As they left the clearing behind them, Melissa was sure she heard the hermit's loud and cackling laugh.

The green swarmed with villagers a little later that morning, more than had gone to the forest. Melissa saw just about everyone she'd met in Fours Crossing, with the exception of Jed's father and, of course, the hermit.

"All right, folks," shouted Mr. Henry Ellison, using his hands for a megaphone. He seemed to be in charge of the procession as he had been of the tree cutting. "It sure doesn't look much like spring-thaw time, but what do we care? We'll show that old weatherman Fours Crossing knows what time of year it is, won't we?"

A cry of "Yes!" peppered with laughter went up from the crowd.

"We've got to get with our own classes," Jed whispered. "I'll see you when it's over, at your gran's."

Melissa nodded, and Jed went across the street to where the eighth grade was standing.

The tree, now strapped upright to the sleigh that Jed had used to get Melissa at the station, was nearly hidden among the cluster of eighth-graders. Melissa knew from what Jed had told her that the procession would be led by the youngest schoolchild in Fours Crossing, Tommy's little cousin Susie. The marchers would be in two long lines, one of schoolchildren in order of classes, working up from the first grade, and the other of everyone else, following the town officials. Between and slightly ahead of them on each side of the sleigh would march the Eights, solemnly guarding the tree; they would present it formally at all the village houses. At the front door of each house, Melissa knew, the two lines of marchers would fall behind the Eights, one line on each side, so that the whole group would form a V with the sleigh-borne tree and Susie at its point. Then would come the singing of the Festival song, and after it the procession would re-form and march to the next house.

A raw wind began to blow as Mr. Ellison mounted the newly shoveled steps at the foot of Bradford Ellison's statue. "All right, folks. You ready, Eights?

Calm down there, you little ones — what are you, Twos? Yes, well, take it easy. . . No, no, it's all right, Mrs. LaSalle. All you teachers, back with the citizens now. Your chicks'll behave, won't you, kids?" There was good-natured laughter from the crowd and a few muffled clucks and crows from the fifth grade. Susie looked very tiny and fragile with her golden hair flowing over the back of a white coat and the coat flowing over spotless white leggings.

Melissa fell into step beside Tommy as the procession moved silently through the village and up the hill toward Gran's, where the ceremonies would start.

"You guys are up to something, aren't you, you and Jed?" whispered Tommy enviously. "Can't I be in it, too?"

"It's not anything, really," Melissa whispered back. "We're not up to anything."

"Oh, come on! You know you are! Jed won't say what it is either." Tommy lowered his voice even more. "That dog's not really Jed's, is he? I mean, not even in a wild way . . ."

"Less talking there in the Sevens," called an authoritative voice from behind them. "We're almost there."

At the top of the hill, right outside Gran's, Mr. Ellison signaled Susie to stop and gestured the schoolchildren to fall back to one side. Mr. Ellison led the townspeople back to the other side, and the V was formed. Then, facing the dining-room window, with the perfect young tree high on the sleigh before them, the villagers gently began the Festival song — and Melissa felt chills all up and down her spine.

Now the cold has gone away,
Deck our tree with flowers gay.
This the tree the year has spared,
This the year that we have shared.

Forest spirit, hear our prayer:
   Bring the springtime!
   Bring the sunshine!
   Bring the bud and bring the leaf!
   Bring the seed and then the sheaf.
Let the warmth our cold hearts thaw
As the snow melts, as the ice melts,
As the birds come, singing, to us,
Snowdrop, crocus, tulip for us;
Lilac, lily, autumn leaf,
Corn, squash, pumpkin, glowing golden—
To spring's coming, we're beholden.
Seasons crossing, turning round,
All four joining, starting now.

Now the cold has gone away,
Deck our tree with flowers gay.
This the tree the year has spared,
This the year that we have shared.

There was silence for a moment when the song
was done. Then Mr. Ellison motioned to Susie and
lifted her up so she could fasten a small white flower
to the top of the tree. It was, Gran had told Melissa
earlier, a snowdrop, forced into bloom indoors for
Festival — though normally, Gran had said, snowdrops were blooming outside before Festival, even
if there was still snow on the ground. Melissa knew
that at each place the procession stopped another
small child would hang a snowdrop on the tree, and
that this year most of them would be paper. At the

90

very end, when the procession returned to Gran's, Susie would be lifted again to the top of the tree, where she would put, next to the first snowdrop, a bright-yellow daffodil, also forced into bloom indoors.

When Susie was back on the ground, the *V* straightened out and the procession wound its way down the hill again and into the village, still singing. The song was repeated over and over as the villagers stopped at each house and farm, until the little tree was heavy with paper flowers.

The wind blew harder as the procession went back up the hill, more slowly this time, because everyone was tired. Several of the eighth-graders, Jed among them, climbed onto the sleigh to steady the tree and to keep the flowers from blowing off in the wind. Melissa saw that Jed's face looked strained and that he kept glancing anxiously up at the sky.

When they stopped outside Gran's dining room this time, a brisk and heavy snow began to fall as if mocking the villagers and their ceremony. The Festival song, so joyous before, sounded grim and sad when they sang it now. The daffodil was limp with cold when Susie placed it at the tree's top. Susie whimpered a little when she was lifted down, and Melissa realized that the child's fingers, bare for fastening the flower, must be stiff and aching with cold.

There was no smile on Mr. Ellison's face as he and Jed lifted the tree carefully down from the sleigh and stood it in the snow outside Gran's dining-room window, where, Tommy whispered, it was placed every year. The paper flowers were fast becoming soggy in the falling snow, and the few real ones drooped forlornly, wilted by the wind.

"Now the cold has gone away," sang the people for the last time as they turned sadly away from Gran's, their voices subdued. "Deck our tree with flowers gay . . ." It was as if no one believed the words any more; Melissa could barely hear them.

Melissa went to stand by Jed, who was near the sleigh. "The cold hasn't gone away," he whispered to her, shivering, "and I'm not sure now it ever will — look." He pointed to the sky, which hung like a thick gray canopy over the village, shutting out the sun.

"This the tree the year has spared," came thinly from the villagers as they moved slowly down the hill. "This the year that we have shared . . ."

Suddenly the air was split with a long, mournful howl that rose to a high note and then broke eerily downward, like a wolf's. The people still on the hill stopped and looked back, huddling together.

"Look," said Jed again.

In the distance, at the edge of the forest but far enough out in the field to be silhouetted against the snow, stood Ulfin, his head thrown back in a second piercing howl that had all of sadness in it.

No one moved till it was over.

"That dog must be part wolf," muttered one of the men. "We'd best tell the dog officer about him."

As if he'd heard, Ulfin wheeled and loped back into the forest.

Jed turned desperate eyes to Melissa. "I said it was as if time had stopped and . . ." He broke off abruptly, staring into Gran's window.

Melissa followed his eyes.

Straight ahead through the glass, directly facing the spot where the tree stood and had been placed for more years than anyone in the village could remember, she saw the pale space on Gran's wall where the fourth plate had hung, and the edges of the other three.

The three were back in their original positions.

9

Melissa and Jed nearly fell over each other in their haste to get into the house. Not stopping to take off their jackets, they flung open the dining-room door and burst inside. "Wait!" Jed shouted as Melissa reached up to take the plates down from the wall. "First we'd better see if there's any sign of someone's getting in here and rearranging them."

But there wasn't.

"Now?" asked Melissa, and Jed nodded.

They put the plates next to each other on the table.

It was as if they both knew exactly what they had to do.

"Look," said Melissa. "A couple of the squiggles are the same as each other, at least sort of." She pointed to a wavy line with a small raised dot to its right on the first plate, and to the same figure, reversed, on the third. "There are two of this one, I think, and" — she pointed again, this time to the two oblongs on the center plate — "two of this. If it *is* a cipher," she said, "that'll help us solve it."

"How come you're so sure it's a cipher?" Jed asked curiously.

She told him about her math class.

"Well," he said, looking dubiously at the plates again, "I suppose cipher is as good a guess as any." Then he brightened. "Hey, look!" he said, pointing. "There are *three* of this one! Look at the two sideways *Y*'s, sort of, here on the last plate. There's another sideways *Y* on the first plate, except it's facing the other way. Hey, I bet you're right, Melissa," he told her excitedly. "I bet it *is* a cipher! I've always thought it's some kind of writing, anyway."

But Melissa was frowning. "I think we should turn the end plate," she said, "to make the sideways *Y* and the dot-and-wavy-line squiggle go the same way as the ones on the first one." She tried it:

and then it was Jed who frowned. "Rats," he said. "Look — the Y's aren't the same at all! But these things" — he pointed to ⅄ — "are. Now what?"

Melissa turned the first plate and then the third, trying to make the sideways Y's match. But it was impossible.

Jed ran his finger back and forth over the two sets of symbols — left to right, right to left, left to right, right to left. "Hey, wait a minute," he said suddenly. "We don't even know what direction the words go in — if the squiggles do spell words."

"We have to assume they do," Melissa said absently, "or we won't get anywhere." Substitution cipher, she was thinking again, in which each symbol stands for a single letter — I *hope* it's that, she thought, and that the letters aren't scrambled, too. If only we had some kind of guide . . .

But we don't, she told herself, watching Jed turn the plates slowly, as if he expected the real letters to be revealed if only he held the plates the right way. "I'm so sure the squiggles mean *something*," he said, frowning, "otherwise why would the hermit have . . ."

"The hermit," Melissa cried, pushing her chair back. "That's it — of course! We do have a guide!" She leaped excitedly to her feet and was partway out

96

of the room before she noticed that Jed was looking at her as if he thought she was crazy. "What guide?" he asked. "What are you talking about?"

"Oh," she said, sheepish now. "The hermit's funny-looking book. I guess I didn't tell you."

"Didn't tell me what? Melissa, you didn't . . ."

Melissa explained quickly how the pages had come out when Jed had taken the hermit's book from her — "almost as if they'd wanted to," she called to Jed as she ran up the stairs.

She came pelting back down almost immediately, waving her small collection of brittle, age-yellowed pages. "Some of the squiggles *are* the same!" she shouted. "Maybe all of them — look — here are these two." She pointed to ⅊ and ⅃ on the first of her pages, and then turned the last plate so those two symbols there matched them:

"Look at this," she went on, back with the book again, pointing to a few lines that were centered at the top of the first page:

"It looks sort of like a poem, doesn't it — or a title — it was the first page in the whole book, I think. Anyway, it looks as if some of the symbols there match some of the ones on the plates. All we have to do is turn the plates a bit . . ." She moved them carefully around till they looked like this:

"And there we are!"

Both she and Jed sat in silence for a few seconds, looking from the plates to the page and back again, both of them checking the symbols, one by one.

"Of course we can't be certain," said Melissa, "but we do have four whole symbols right here on this page that are also on the first plate. And look," she said, after another few minutes, "here are your Y-looking things in the book — two different ones, which is why we couldn't get all three of the ones on the plates to match." She looked up at him in triumph.

But Jed seemed unconvinced. "Now all we have to do," he said gloomily, "is figure out how to get letters and words out of the squiggles, right?"

Melissa nodded and then ran into the kitchen for a pencil and a pad of paper. Jed might be good at woodchopping and grammar and snowshoeing; he might read a lot and have a fine-daydreamer's imagination, but it was going to take solid scientific persistence to break this cipher — for she was certain now that it was one — and that was just the kind of persistence Melissa knew she had.

When she got back to the dining room, this is what she wrote down:

∞ (1)   ♁ (1)   ⤫ (1)   Ɣ (2)

～ (1)   ɤ (2)   ſ (1)   △ (1)

Ɣ (1)   ⊥ (2)   ⴱ (2)   ⤫ (1)

"The numbers are how many times they're on the plates," she explained. "I'm not sure if we'll need that or not, but it's supposed to be important to know which letters — which symbols — are used the most. Let's see if we can find the rest of the plate symbols in the book, and then let's write down whatever other symbols are in the book — symbols that aren't on the plates, I mean. If we're lucky," she added, "we'll end up with twenty-six different squiggles."

Jed made a noise halfway between a snort and a laugh. "I can't believe spies do it this way," he grumbled. "It'll only take us about twelve years *after* we find the whole alphabet to figure out which letter's which. Melissa, do you realize that any one symbol could stand for any one of the twenty-six letters?"

"Umm-hmm," said Melissa, "but that's still only twenty-six possibilities at the most for each one. Fewer each time you guess one right."

Jed shook his head and reached across Melissa for the plates. "You go ahead with that," he said. "I'm going to see what I can figure out from the plates themselves." He ran his finger along the L-shaped groove in one of them. "I just can't believe they're really plates. Why would anyone put something like this on a plate?"

Melissa shrugged and continued to hunt through the handwritten pages, trying to assemble twenty-six different symbols, while Jed took the plates to the other end of the table, frowning in deep concentration.

When I've found twenty-six, Melissa thought, making a list on her pad, I'll still have to check further to make sure there aren't any more than that. But wait, she thought, even if there are, some could be numbers — but that would only be nine more — no, ten, with a zero if it's the same number system as ours — so if I find more than thirty-six symbols, she told herself, I'll know I'm wrong.

But after an hour's hunting, Melissa had found only twenty-six symbols after all, and she proudly showed her "alphabet" to Jed:

100

"Okay," he said with cautious admiration, "but — I hate to say it — but now what?"

"Now the real work starts," Melissa said with more relish than she actually felt; she was tired. "Next we try to figure out words by putting the symbols together. You're right about spies." She sighed. "But I don't know any other way to go about it."

"Well, you've come up with more than I have anyway," Jed said, giving her shoulder a quick pat. "About all I've figured out so far is that if you turn these silly things different ways, you can make the grooves form a cross — or they would form one if we had all four, and if they were on top of each other and transparent or something. I mean, you can't see easily that they make a cross when they're next to each other, but . . ."

Melissa felt her tiredness melt away as if it had never been. "Fours Crossing!" she shouted, reaching for the plates to see if he was right.

"Huh?"

"Cross — four — Fours Crossing — the name of the village, don't you see?" Excitedly, Melissa laid the plates out on the table the way they'd first hung on the wall — Jed was right that the grooves on each formed a different quarter of a cross, with one quarter missing. "Look," she said, "the letters always go in between two sides of a groove. And — Jed? When the plates are this way, the symbols still go in the direction we thought. That must prove something!"

They both stared down at them.

"If the missing plate were where it belonged," said Jed, his voice a little hushed, "it would probably make the fourth quarter of the cross. I mean, there's no reason to think it wouldn't . . ."

"And," said Melissa, "the whole thing must mean that the plates — four, with a cross — have something very special to do with the village."

"Melissa," said Jed generously, "has anyone told you that you might just possibly be a genius?"

She grinned. "No one," she said, "but you might mention it to Miss Laurent. I don't think I did too well on the last English test. Math, now . . ."

"I still don't see how they can really be plates," said Jed, "except I don't see what else they could be."

"Neither do I."

Jed reached for Melissa's papers. "Well, that's what this whole alphabet hunt's been for, right? To figure it out. We might as well get back to work. But how?" he said, idly writing a large *A* next to the first symbol and a *B* next to the second.

"No, no," said Melissa, tearing a fresh piece of paper off her pad. "Not like that. This part I do know about," she said, "a little, anyway. What you do is, you look for easy words — for one- and two- and three-letter words. And for double letters, and letters that there are lots of — things like that." She pulled the book closer. "Let's start with one-letter words . . ."

"*I* and *A*," said Jed excitedly. "I get it. I bet *I* and *A* are the only one-letter words in English!" He took the book from Melissa. "Here we are," he said almost immediately, pointing. "Write this one down. Holy cow, it's even in that title or whatever it is!"

In a large bold hand Melissa wrote:

$$\text{☜} = I \text{ or } A$$

And a few seconds later, Jed wrote:

$$\text{ʒ} = I \text{ or } A$$

"Now let's look for *E*," said Melissa. "My math teacher told us that's the most common letter in English. Come on, Jed, *count*!"

Half an hour later, they had two candidates for *E* — ⅃ and △.

"Now what?" asked Jed, leaning back in his chair.

"Well," Melissa said doubtfully, "I think *T*'s the most common after *E*, and *A* after that. We'll just have to count, and then experiment — try to make two- and three-letter words out of the letters we think we have — that kind of thing. I can't think of any other way," she said apologetically.

Jed smiled grimly. "Well — as you said — let's count."

After two more hours of meticulous hunting, with Melissa remembering more and more from her math class, they finally had this:

⊕ = T
▯ = H
⅃ = E

⊛ = I
ⵒ = A

ⴽ = S
y = N

△ = O

Ɛ = ?

⊕▯⅃
T H E

⊕▯ⵒⴽ⊕
T H A T

⊛ ⴽ   ⊕▯ⵒy
I S   T H A N

⊛ y   ⊕▯⅃y
I N   T H E N

△y   ⊕△   △y⊕△
ON   TO   ONTO

⊛y⊕△
INTO

"Look," Jed shouted suddenly, "we've got all the letters for this word." He wrote down ⴽ⅃Ɛⴽ△yⴽ from the book's title and then under it put each letter according to the list they had made so far.

"Wow!" said Melissa. She felt as much like hugging him now as she'd felt like shaking him earlier. But then the impact of what they'd found hit both of them, and they looked at the paper in uncomfortable silence.

ⴽ⅃Ɛⴽ△yⴽ
S E A S O N S

At last Jed whistled low through his teeth. "That sure does tell us something," he said softly.

"It sure does." Melissa found her eyes pulled to the window, to the gloomy, persistent snow.

"I wonder . . ." Jed examined the plates again. "Melissa," he said, after studying the leaf patterns, "look. They make sense when they go the way the cross and the letters go. You can see they're real leaves."

Melissa looked, but living in Boston hadn't taught her much about leaves. They still looked more like decorations to her than anything important.

"Hemlock," said Jed suddenly, pointing to the pattern on the first plate. "It's very stylized, but those little branch things could be hemlock — an artist's idea of it, anyway. And these could be rowan leaves." He pointed to the third plate. "And the other's oak, I bet, more or less."

"Hemlock," said Melissa, interested now. "Christmas trees — four seasons — the Christmas season — winter!"

Jed nodded slowly. "Let's see. Oak leaves — they stay on late in the fall." He counted the cipher letters. "Four."

Melissa laughed nervously. "How about the — what was it you said? row-something?"

"Rowan. Flowers in spring. Berries in — well, late summer, sort of. Flowers in summer, actually. Late spring, early summer . . ."

"Six letters," said Melissa, reaching for her pencil. "Summer."

But the second letter on that plate was △ — the symbol they'd found for O.

"Well," said Jed, a little doubtfully, "the plates are old — maybe it's old-fashioned spelling. Like in some versions of Shakespeare and old poems and things."

"Okay," said Melissa. "Good idea." She wrote down:

>< △ℽℽ⅃ ͻ
S O M M E R

"Does that work as an old spelling?"

"I think so," Jed answered, frowning. "Except I'd have thought only one *M* — oh, I don't know! Let's go on." He picked up the hemlock plate. "This one ought to be winter," he said, "and it's the right number of letters. But — here we go again — the second one isn't an *I*, at least if we've found the right squiggle for *I*."

"How about *Y*?" suggested Melissa, looking over his shoulder. "Wouldn't that sound the same when it was pronounced — W-Y-N-T-E-R?"

In a few more minutes they had it:

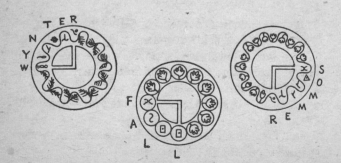

"It's spring that's missing," Jed said quietly when they had finished. "Oh, Melissa. Holy cow."

By the time Gran called from the kitchen to ask why they hadn't had any lunch, Melissa and Jed were sitting exhausted at the paper-littered table staring at what they'd added to their final copy of everything so far. They'd had to guess at a few letters, and they still had one blank — but even so, what they had made perfect sense:

⨯△▽ᴗ⨯   ∧ᴗ△⨯⨯ᴕ⅄↑   ⊙ᴕᔑᴗ~   △⨯
F O U R S   C R O S S I N G   I A R Y   O F

               ⨯△▽ᴗ
               F O U R

               ⨯⅂ᔑ⨯△⅄⨯
               S E A S O N S

"Diary," Melissa said suddenly, pointing to the word. "You said the book looked like the ones people buy for diaries, remember?"

"Right." Jed carefully wrote a *D* in the proper place. "Well," he said. "Now we know."

Melissa wrote silently on her pad: S ⨯ P ᴗR ᴕI ⅄N ↑G

Then she wrote: S ⨯ P ᴗR ~ᴕ⅄ ⅄N ↑G

and: S
       X   P
         ⌐R
         ⌐Y
          Y N
          ↑G
       ⌐E

Jed leaned his chair back, balancing it like a rocker on its rear legs. "It all fits," he said, fingering the pad. "The plates, the hermit, the book, the weather — everything. Even if it's hard to see exactly what the connection is."

"But," Melissa said uncomfortably, "there can't really be a connection at all, can there?"

"Those silver — *things* — have always hung in this spot in this house in this village," Jed said in a low voice. "In Fours Crossing. You said yourself that might mean something. And think of the Festival song: "Seasons *crossing*, turning round,' it says. 'All *four* joining, starting now.' And the book's about seasons — well, it seems to be, anyway." He leaned forward. "Melissa, what gave me the idea to look at the plates again was that the Spring Festival tree's always held up to this window, in a direct line from where the missing plate — the spring plate — hung. I still can't quite figure out why, but . . ."

Jed led Melissa to the front door, and opened it.

The sky was still dark, dark enough for twilight, though it was not yet even four o'clock in the afternoon. Snow fell lazily but steadily, as if it were never going to stop, and the roads were again impassable except by sleigh or snowshoe. The buds on the big viburnum bush outside Gran's front door were still so tightly rolled they were barely visible, and if the snowdrops near the front path had come up at all, they were probably rotting now under the snow that buried them. A single dry oak leaf scudded across the snow's surface, and under one of Gran's feeders a thin squirrel foraged weakly for bird seed, so hungry it didn't seem to notice Melissa and Jed only a few feet away. Gran's paths were like canyons, the snow was piled thickly on the henhouse roof again, and there were no icicles anywhere now, because there had been no melting, not even from the house's heat.

"Melissa," came Jed's voice in the darkness, "I know Fours Crossing isn't your village. But it's your Gran's house where the plate hung, and it's her dining-room window Ulfin always sits under. Your window, too, since your room's just above the dining room. Melissa, Ulfin never came here till you did — he seems — to want you — to think it's your job, too. I'll help — but you — *we* — have got to get the fourth plate back again. If we don't — Melissa, what if nothing's ever green in Fours Crossing again?"

10

It isn't, Melissa thought off and on all the next day as she struggled to write an English composition, that Fours Crossing isn't my village. It isn't that at all. She knew she was close to liking Fours Crossing more than she'd ever liked Boston. Certainly she liked Jed more than anyone her own age she'd ever known.

But what does that mean? she wondered, putting her aching head down on the desk in her room and closing her eyes. Did I never know *how* to have a friend before — except Mumma?

Memories flooded her:

Her mother in her light-blue dress, smiling, leading five-year-old Melissa past cages in the zoo, giggling with her over the monkey who had just tossed a package of nuts back to a boy who'd thrown it at him . . .

Her mother, before Melissa went to sleep, sitting on the edge of her bed, listening when she was tiny to her God-bless-Daddy-and-Mumma prayers; when she was older to the events of her day, to anything, anything at all that troubled her . . .

Did I ever listen to Mumma? I listen to Jed . . .

Her mother, in springtime, walking all over Beacon Hill with Melissa, hunting for the first crocus. They always found it in Mrs. Halliday's dooryard, and it was always blue . . .

Spring again. Why did it always have to come back to that?

She picked up the cipher pages from where they were lying on her desk next to her unfinished composition. But then she stuffed them inside her desk drawer. She'd never get her homework done if she tried to read them, never.

It was the next afternoon at school that light-headedness and a sore throat added themselves to Melissa's headache and out-of-sorts feeling of the day before. She'd had to stay up late finishing and copying over her composition, and she'd done a lot of yelling in gym that morning, but she'd agreed to go to the library with Jed that afternoon, so there was no question of going home early.

"I thought," Jed told her as they plodded along the edge of the green that afternoon, "that we could try looking up Spring Festival. Maybe that'll tell us something. There's a pretty good collection of books on town history, and a few on folklore — there might be something in them about it. Which do you want? Melissa?"

"What? Oh — folklore, I guess." She realized it was getting harder and harder to concentrate; she felt as if she weren't really there, somehow, or as if she were on the other side of the green, watching herself walk beside Jed.

"You okay?" he asked. "You sound kind of funny."

"Sore throat," she said, using as few words as possible. "Maybe a cold. Folklore's fine."

"Everybody's getting sick," Jed said gloomily as they went around the church to the library entrance in the back. "Mr. Titus — he runs the general store? He said he's just about out of aspirin and nose drops and cough syrup now, along with food and stuff. What I wouldn't give for a chocolate bar — oh, well." Jed undid his snowshoes and stood them up against the side of the building. "We'll know it's really bad, I guess, the day we leave our snowshoes out for just a couple of hours and come back to find them buried."

Melissa managed a smile, and they went inside.

Jed nodded at the elderly white-haired librarian who quietly said hello to them as they passed her desk and then he whispered to Melissa, making her smile again, "Her name's Ellison — of course."

The library was one big room, but it seemed small to Melissa; you could, she thought, fit it about five times just in the concourse of the Boston Public in Copley Square. Tables and shelves cleverly divided the room into cozy sections. Melissa had to admit that with its dark woodwork, bright curtains, and the glowing warmth from its wood-burning stove, it was the most cheerful-looking library she'd ever seen, and the homiest, even if it was small.

Jed pointed out the folklore section — about a quarter of one short shelf — and went himself to the slightly longer section marked TOWN HISTORY.

Melissa read for nearly an hour before she found anything that seemed to have anything at all to do with what they were looking for. Some of it was interesting, but it was hard to pay attention. Her mind was just starting to float comfortably back to Gran's when her eye fell on something on the page she'd just turned and she froze.

There was an account of a spring procession very like the one in Fours Crossing.

True, it was held on May Day, and true, it had been celebrated in Europe, not America — but still, there was no denying the similarity:

In many European countries an old custom persists on the first of May of cutting a tree from the nearby woods and carrying it from house to house through the village. The origin of this is religious, perhaps lying in the pagan belief that a woods spirit, dwelling in the tree, has the power to grant luck, health, and prosperity for the coming season of growth. Or perhaps it is a way of "taking" spring, believed to arrive first in one certain sacred place, to another place.

Her vagueness shocked away, Melissa got up and went to Jed, who was deep in the thick book open in front of him. *A History of Fours Crossing*, Melissa read at the top of the page he was reading.

She stood there a moment, waiting, but he was so absorbed he didn't seem to notice. "Jed," she whispered finally, "Jed, I think I've found something."

He looked up slowly, frowning. "Huh?"

She put her book down on top of his, open to the paragraph about the first of May.

"It fits," he murmured a minute later, nodding. "You're right — you did find something." For just a fraction of a second he seemed excited, but then he moved her book away and held up his, pointing to the bottom of a left-hand page where there were a few lines under the heading "Early Religious Customs":

In the early days [Melissa read], under the leadership of Eli Dunn, the residents of Fours Crossing village probably worshipped as had their forebears. This may well have involved ancient . . .

That was the end of the page; Melissa's eyes shifted automatically to the page opposite. But what it said there didn't make any sense:

114

use as the turning point the year 1725, the year marking both the end of Eli Dunn and the building, under the supervision of the Reverend Bradford Ellison, of the First Church of Fours Crossing.

And that was all there was of the chapter on religious customs. Puzzled, Melissa read the account again. Why did it say "end" like that? Why not "death" — if that was what it meant? Of course Gran had said — what *was* it she'd said? The more Melissa tried to concentrate, the more her head hurt.

"Look." Jed showed her the thin hard edge of several cutoff paper sheets between where the two pages disappeared into the book's binding. "And look." He pointed to the page numbers. The one on the left was 286; the one on the right, 293.

Melissa fingered the paper edges. "Cut," she said in surprise. "But why . . .?"

"I don't know." Jed looked grim. "And this is the only copy; I already checked that — so we'll never know. But someone must have had a reason for cutting those pages out . . ." He shook his head. "Melissa, remember what your grandmother said about old Eli Dunn? That people thought there was some kind of accident but no one really knew what happened to him when he — disappeared? She used the word 'died,' I think, but . . ." He quickly flipped over pages. "I think there's a list of all the births and deaths for each year. Yes." He scanned the page he'd found and then pushed the book over to Melissa. "See — after each name it says how the person died. But look at this:"

Died

Clarinda Mercy Brown, age 21, February,
    in childbirth
Charity Beckwith, age 3, April, of a quinsy
Seth Beckwith, age 7, April, of a quinsy
Jean Cameron, age 50, November, of Age
Emilie Charbonneau, age 18, August, in childbirth
Eli Dunn
Donald Ellison, age 35, May, of a fall from his
    hayloft

"No reason," said Jed. "No age, no month — as
if they didn't really even want to mention it. Or —
again as if they had something to hide. It doesn't
really even say he died, except of course that his
name's there, so he must have. But . . ." Abruptly
Jed thrust the books back into their places on the
shelves. Then he bent down to where Melissa still
sat supporting her aching head with one hand and
said gently, "Melissa? The only thing I can think of
is to ask Mrs. Titus — she's the Town Clerk —
about Eli Dunn's death, I mean. Maybe it's not important, but — well, if it isn't, I don't see why it's
so mysterious! The Town Clerk's got all the official
birth and death records for each year, along with
Town Meeting records and police records and everything. Maybe she'll let us have a look at 1725 — it's
really the only thing I can think of doing. Melissa —
okay?" He studied her face anxiously.

Tiredly, Melissa pulled herself up. No, she wanted
to say, it's not okay, I want to go home to bed. But
then she wondered if she was being reluctant because

she didn't feel well, or if it was because she didn't want to explore any of this any more — because the more mysterious it became, the more her feeling of dread grew. But that isn't fair to Jed, she told herself, not when I said I'd help, and especially not now that he's said he'll help me . . .

Maybe that's the truest reason, she thought, knowing that she was still very conscious of his saying that it looked as if it was her job, when it was a job she didn't want.

But then the library door opened and several people came in. A blast of cold air burst in that was so much stronger than the warmth from the wood-burning stove that the stove might just as well not have been there. Melissa felt herself shiver.

"Snowdrops," Jed whispered. "Daffodils. Warm rain. Seeds in the ground, grass instead of snow — sunshine."

A child sneezed violently, then sneezed again, three times.

"Melissa." Jed picked up her jacket. "We've *got* to."

The Town Clerk's office was on the second floor of the general store, next to the Selectmen's office. The Town Clerk herself, Mrs. Titus, was so tiny she was almost hidden behind the stacks of paper and the thick ledgers and books on her desk — and so old Melissa found herself thinking she almost might remember what had happened back in 1725.

The records for before 1900, Mrs. Titus explained in a quavery little voice, were stored down in the cellar on shelves Jed's own father had built for the town — but no, she went on, pushing back her too-big chair and hopping spryly around to their side of the desk, no, of course they could see them; she'd be delighted to dig them out — was this a project for school?

"Well, no, not exactly," Jed told her. "Just some — independent research."

"How *nice*!" Mrs. Titus smiled brightly, the wrinkles in her winter-weathered cheeks deepening till her face made Melissa think of a small pale walnut. "It's so *nice* to see young people taking an interest in town history." She reached up to pat Jed's shoulder and then scurried downstairs.

Jed stared moodily out the window while she was gone; Melissa, whose head was beginning to spin dizzily now as well as ache, sank down on the cushioned seat of the large wooden visitor's chair next to Mrs. Titus's desk. An old-fashioned mahogany clock ticked loudly on a shelf across the room. Ten minutes went by — fifteen — twenty.

Then at last they heard Mrs. Titus's steps on the stairs as she came up much more slowly than she'd gone down — heavily, as if she had tired herself out with looking.

The door opened slowly and Mrs. Titus came in, her eyes almost hidden in a deep frown as she looked at Jed and then at Melissa. Her little ink-stained fingers fluttered nervously as she spoke. "I don't understand it," she muttered, as if only half aware of them now. "I thought I knew all those old records inside and out, top, bottom, and sideways. I can't imagine never noticing — I just can't imagine!"

Jed glanced at Melissa and then asked, "Not noticing what, Mrs. Titus? What is it you didn't notice?"

"Why," she said in astonishment, "not noticing that there *are* no records for 1725! No records at all!" Mrs. Titus sat down heavily at her desk, still shaking her head. "You'll have to pick another year for your project, children, I'm afraid. I just don't understand, though, I just can't imagine . . ."

". . . No records whatsoever," Melissa heard Mrs. Titus still muttering after she and Jed had thanked her and were going dejectedly back down the stairs. "None whatsoever at all!"

11

The next morning Melissa's headache was worse and her throat felt as if it were on fire. She had dreamed of her mother that night for the first time in quite a while, but the dream was mixed up with the plates and the hermit and a stern minister who looked like Jed and kept pointing an accusing finger at the hermit, who could almost have been her own father grown old and very crusty. It had seemed confused and distorted when she'd dreamed it, and now, as she tried to find the energy to brush her hair and dress for school, it seemed all wrong, oddly jumbled like so much else this cold and snowy winter.

And like the pages of the cipher book, which were still stuffed away in her desk drawer, and which had hovered over her head in her dream like strange, demanding birds.

At breakfast, Gran seemed unusually brisk. She had made scrambled eggs because someone in the village had canceled their usual egg order, and to go with them had baked muffins. Normally, Melissa would have wolfed the meal down, glad of the change from their usual weekday porridge (which powdered milk did nothing to improve), but this morning she ate listlessly, her heavy aching head supported on one hand and the other hand loosely holding a fork with which she could only pick at her food.

"Aren't you hungry?" Gran asked, sitting down opposite her. "My goodness, I could still eat a horse, even though all that marching was back on Saturday! Did Miss Laurent like your composition, by the way?"

"I don't know," Melissa said indifferently. "I guess I'll get it back today."

"Don't you feel well, lambie?" Gran asked, getting up and putting a cool hand on Melissa's head. "My land, child!" she exclaimed, "you're burning up! Back to bed with you, my girl, while I call Dr. Ellison."

Melissa heard herself giggling weakly at the name — of course it would be Ellison — and she gratefully let Gran lead her back upstairs. It hadn't occurred to her that she was really sick, outside of having a slight cold. But of course that was why she'd been feeling so strange, and now all she'd have to do was lie in bed and not even think, especially not about spring and plates that might not be plates at all, or about Dunns or Ellisons or what happened way back in 1725 — nothing, she said to herself fuzzily, undressing; it's all going to go away and I'm going to be better in a few days, like waking up from a bad dream — none of it will have happened. Realizing only dimly that didn't quite make sense, Melissa crept back between the covers and immediately fell asleep.

She woke only partway when Dr. Ellison, an elderly, grandfatherly sort of man, came and examined her briefly. She dozed while he stood in the doorway talking to Gran, saying the usual doctor things: "Lots of it going around . . . some kind of flu . . . too much bad weather . . . plenty of rest . . . fluids . . . light meals . . . fruit juices . . . keep her warm . . . aspirin for the fever . . . look in tomorrow . . . half the village has it, Mrs. Dunn, don't worry."

Melissa closed her eyes again and dreamed that her mother was sitting by her bed, bathing her forehead with a soft cool cloth. When she woke, it was to see Gran beside her; she put her head in Gran's lap and felt tears sting her eyes. But they still didn't spill over, not even when Gran gently stroked her shoulder and then smoothed her hair back off her forehead. "Poor little mite," said Gran softly, "you really feel punk, don't you?" Gently Gran moved Melissa back onto the pillow. "Why, it almost looks as if there are tears in your eyes, child, what is it?"

Melissa shook her head; she was too tired to explain she had thought for a moment that her mother was with her, and she realized even through her fever that it might hurt Gran to know.

But Gran seemed to understand, anyway. She kissed Melissa's forehead and said, "You miss your mother, lambie, don't you?" She sighed. "I wish you'd talk about her."

Melissa closed her eyes.

Gran sighed again and stood up. "I'm going to get myself a cup of tea," she said quietly, "and feed the birds — even the crows look thin now, poor raucous things, though how any birds survive at all in such weather I'll never know. Then I'll just put some soup on for your supper and be right back up."

Melissa tried to nod but had to stop midway, her head and neck ached so. Maybe I'm dying, she thought without fear as Gran left, and then she fell asleep again. This time she dreamed that she and her mother, dressed in long blue gowns and with pale-blue wings coming from their shoulders, were chasing clouds across the sky as if they were errant sheep. They even had a cloud dog, a beautiful pale-gold animal with a golden collar and a golden name tag . . .

"Just a few swallows, lambie, just to give you a little strength. And a sip of this nice fizzy grape juice. Your daddy called; he says he loves you and he hopes you'll feel better soon. The grape juice is from him — he told me you like grape juice with ginger ale."

Melissa sat up partway, supported by Gran's arm, and gulped the juice down gratefully, though swallowing still hurt her throat. She had never been so thirsty. The soup was as hot as she was, so she didn't want it, but the juice was wonderful. Daddy, had Gran said?

Gran nodded. "He sends his love and wishes he were here with you, and he's sorry he hasn't written much. He said to tell you he once carried the tree for Spring Festival, when he was in the eighth grade."

"Did it thaw?" Melissa asked sleepily. She did feel a little better — maybe it was the juice.

"Oh, yes," said Gran softly. "Certainly. It did the year your daddy carried the tree, and it has every year I know about, except this one."

Melissa closed her eyes and leaned back again. She knew that; of course it hadn't thawed this year, how could it, with the plate stolen and in the hands of that strangely mad relative of hers up in the woods?

Her eyes flew open for a moment, startled at how easily the thought had fluttered into her mind, like the cipher-page birds in her dream the night before, *Stop* it, she told herself angrily; it's only because you're sick that you thought that. Spring's because of the earth's rotation, because of . . .

But thinking scientifically made her headache worse.

In the next minute Melissa found herself trying to get up to take the cipher pages out of her drawer. She did manage to sit up, but then she fell back onto her pillow, too dizzy to even try to put her feet on the floor.

There is no such thing as magic; no such thing as a set of silver plates that can control the seasons, she repeated over and over to herself as her eyes closed in restless sleep.

Melissa stayed in bed all week, most of the time with Pride and Joy purring contentedly at her feet. It wasn't until late Saturday afternoon when Gran was busy cooking dinner that she felt well enough to look at the cipher pages again.

The first thing she did was to write out a fresh, neat list of all the symbols they'd deciphered so far — eighteen, in all, more than half. Finding just eight more shouldn't be hard at all! She picked up the title page, easily filled in most of the missing letters in a short three-line section they hadn't deciphered earlier — and then she stared in disbelief at the name that, though incomplete, seemed to stare back up at her:

⤬△▽⤳⤬   Λ⤳△⤬⤬⥾Ɣↈ   ☉⥾ʔⱲ⤳ △⤬
FOURS   CROSSING   DIARY OF

⤬△▽Ⱳ
FOUR

⤳Λʔ⤬△Ɣ⤬
SEASONS

ɎⱲ
Y

ʔↃⱢɎ ☉▽ɎɎ
E EN DUNN

◊☉ΛΛ▱▱♭
MDCC

125

Could that really be true? Could it really be . . . ?
⟨ ᷧ had to spell *by*.

And that meant that . . .

Melissa just had time to slide the diary pages and her pad of paper under the covers when Gran came in with both their dinners on a big tray. She wanted to show the papers to Gran and explain to her what she and Jed were doing — but I can't do that without asking, Jed, she decided reluctantly.

That didn't mean, though, that she couldn't ask Gran a question or two, just to verify what she was thinking.

"My, you're looking better!" Gran said as she put Melissa's plate and glass on the small bed tray that was already across her knees. "Do you feel as much better as you look?"

"Almost," Melissa said; she still had a headache and her throat was still a little sore. "Gran," she asked as casually as she could when Gran was seated in the doorway with her own dinner on a small table, "what was the name of that boy — old Eli Dunn's son, I mean, that you told us about on the night of the blizzard?"

Gran looked surprised. "Eben Dunn, you mean? The one who married Tabitha Ellison?"

"Yes, that's the one." Melissa began to cut her chicken, trying to distract herself from the sudden frenzied beating of her heart.

Gran spooned gravy over one of the biscuits she'd made to go with dinner. "About all I know of him," she said, "is what I've already told you — that he

126

kept trying to convince old Eli to move back to the village but couldn't, and that he married Tabitha." She chuckled. "I don't think Eben Dunn ever did anything much at all except marry Tabitha — and became Forest Keeper, of course, after old Eli was gone."

"And no one knows," Melissa said carefully, "what happened to Eli, right?"

"Right. Leastways, no one that I know of." Gran smiled. "Goodness, child, are you thinking of writing the family history?"

Melissa smiled back. "No," she said. "No, Jed and I were just looking up some town history, that's all, and — well, whoever wrote what we read didn't seem to know what had happened to Eli, either."

Somehow that rather vague answer seemed to satisfy Gran, but Melissa could hardly wait to get back to the "Diary of Four Seasons." All through the rest of dinner, and all through the long evening while she and Gran watched a movie on Gran's portable TV set, her thoughts kept turning back to Eben: if it was his diary, why had he written it in cipher? And why did the hermit have it now? And why had it been in the oak chest along with the two strange robes, one so old it crumbled and the other so new it looked as if it had hardly been worn?

But despite all her unanswered and, she feared, maybe unanswerable questions, Melissa was still sick enough to tire easily. When the movie ended and Gran yawned and said, "My goodness, I'm nearly asleep — you are, too, lambie, from the look of you," she realized she was too worn out and head-achy to do any more deciphering. By the next after-noon, though, Melissa felt better enough to get out the diary again, and her pad, and the pencils she'd sharpened the day before.

Seven more letters to go, she told herself, filling in the *B*'s in *by* and *Eben*. Then she turned to the diary itself and began writing letters under all the symbols she knew. It should be easy, she reasoned, to guess most of the missing seven just by filling in the blanks in words — like a crossword puzzle, she thought, turning back to the first page and adding a *J* to the word

ANUAR Y

which was in the upper-right-hand corner. ▭▭▭, she said to herself, must be a date — January some-thing. But how can a date like that be written in three symbols?

There must be something wrong, she thought, turning back to the title page, where she still had ▭▭▵ to decipher at the end of the last word.

The symbol ▭, she realized, skimming the other diary pages, seemed to appear in only two other places, one of which was only three letters long: ✕ ꝛ ▭ —but ▵, the other undeciphered symbol F I
on the title page, appeared three times in the very first paragraph:

$$□ \, \backsim \, ? \, \otimes \, \curlywedge \, \backsim$$
H E A I E

$$\backsim \, \omega \, \curlywedge \, \boxminus \, \boxminus$$
E I L L

$$\backsim \, \omega \, \backsim \, \curlywedge$$
E E R

It didn't take her long to realize that only one of the letters she wasn't already sure of — *V* — made any sense at all in all three of those words:

$$□ \, \backsim \, ? \, \otimes \, \curlywedge \, \backsim$$
H E A V I E

$$\backsim \, \omega \, \curlywedge \, \boxminus \, \boxminus$$
E V I L L

$$\backsim \, \omega \, \backsim \, \curlywedge$$
E V E R

Well, she reasoned, if old-fashioned spelling was used on the plates, maybe it was used in the diary, too. Good — but then after she'd successfully filled in a few more symbols, she went back to the title page and put a *V* for the ⌂ in the last word. And all that gave her was ⟨⊙∧∧◻◻⌂ — which

       M D C C   V

still didn't seem to make any sense.

Melissa closed her eyes and leaned back, listening to the shoveling sounds from outside. Then, ignoring her pounding head as best she could, she doggedly counted up the symbols she had now, including the ones she'd guessed at.

Twenty-four! That meant—

That meant the only two letters she didn't have definite symbols or near-definite symbols for were *X* and *Z*.

And you almost gave up, Melissa Dunn, she scolded herself, hunting through the paragraph again for the one word she knew had the symbol ◁ in it. There it was, about two-thirds of the way down the page:

"Fiz?" she said aloud, doubtfully, making Pride and Joy look up from the elaborate bath he was now taking at the foot of her bed. "Or fix? Fix!"

It didn't completely make sense with the rest of the sentence, but it made enough sense. More than fiz, anyway.

January ZZZ didn't make any sense — but neither did January XXX.

And neither, she thought, writing them down, did MDCCZZV or MDCCXXV.

She leaned back, discouraged again — but then snapped forward, staring. MDCCXXV suddenly looked oddly familiar. Like — like . . .

Of course!

Melissa pushed back the covers, displacing a very surprised Pride and Joy, and leaped out of bed.

January XXX had to be a date; that was clear. And dates, she told herself, have to be numbers in some form or other. But there are only twenty-six symbols in this cipher alphabet — and that, she wanted to shout aloud, means that anyone who wants to encipher a number has to spell it out. Or use letters in some way . . .

Melissa ran to her desk and flipped eagerly through the pages in the big dictionary Gran had put there to help her with her schoolwork.

And then she stood still, looking down at the page.

XXX, of course, as she'd suddenly realized, was 30 in Roman numerals.

And the dictionary confirmed that MDCCXXV was 1725.

12

"Holy cow!" Jed said the next day. "Holy, holy cow!"

He had just delivered Melissa's homework and was standing beside her bed, reading the
papers she held out to him — first the complete
cipher alphabet:

⌇- A	▣-H	△-O	৪-V
Ɣ- B	ᴈ- I	<- J... wait

(cipher symbols)

Symbol	Letter	Symbol	Letter	Symbol	Letter	Symbol	Letter
⌇	A	▣	H	△	O	৪	V
Ɣ	B	ᴈ	I	⌇	P	∞	W
∧	C	<	J	Ȥ	Q	⊏	X
☉	D	⌇	K	∿	R	∾	Y
⊥	E	⊟	L	✕	S	⌒	Z
✕	F	√	M	✧	T		
↑	G	Y	N	▽	U		

And then the important part of the first of the two
diary fragments that she'd spent the day deciphering. Some of the spelling was inconsistent, and of

course she'd had to guess at punctuation, but that hadn't been too difficult. The only hard part was that some words that should have ended in *-ed*, especially in the last section, seemed to have the *e*'s missing; she decided to put apostrophes in those places where the *e*'s should have been.

This is what Melissa handed Jed:

January 30

It is with a heavie Hand and sore that I, Eben Dunn, take up my Pen to commence this sad Account. I know not why I feel this premonition of Evill, but it is so strong that I feel I must fix this Account, what ever it may tell, in the Old Letters, so that only our Familie may read it.

For now, I knowe not what ails my poor Father, Eli Dunn, and it is for Feare of him that I write this and record his strange Wayes. He is spendyng a bleake and barren Wynter again I feare, still self exiled in the house he built by the Saw Mill, the sadder in that Tabitha and I are snugge and joyous in the Village, as joyous as is possible with this dark Dread that fills me unto Pannick. It is true that Loneliness suits my Father. As Leader both in civil Matters and in the Ceremonies, it was of course long his Lot to be aloof. It is not that. It is the Bitterness that I see growe in him, the Pain that seems to fill him more and more. He murmurs of Betrayal, and he has still not permitted my Tabitha to cross the Thresh hold of his House. The last time we try'd to visit him, he threw a Stone at her Dogg, the pup I gave her from my Father's dog's own Litter, grazing our Dog's Shoulder painfully and bringing tears to my dear Tabitha's Eyes. Our poor Ulfin. He is the gentlest of Beastes . . .

"Holy cow!" said Jed again. "This is — Melissa, is there any more?"

She nodded, although since she'd finished her deciphering, she, like Eben, had been feeling a growing sense of "dark Dread."

"There's a bit more from the beginning," she said, "but it's just about how glad he is to be married to Tabitha and about how they plan to add to their house in the village. But then there's this. I guess it's from pretty close to the end." She handed him the remaining page:

> May 3, continued
>
> ... from the Forest of Winter," my poor demented Father shouted at us all, assembl'd there as we were in the Grove's Temple. And then tho it pains me sore to say it he rais'd the Circlet as a Weapon, to strike me, his Son. Had not the blessed Dogg thrust himself between us, clattering the Circlet to the stoney floor, I know not what would have been my Fate, nor if I ever again should have held my sweet Tabitha in my Armes.
>
> It is then that my Father, knock'd also to the Floor and reeling, grop'd his way from stone to stone like some Prehistoric Worme, some mythic Dragon, some Phoenix born of Death. For then, before our Eyes, I swear it, he mouth'd weakly Wordes that seem'd to say I will return and then, on a sudden strengthened, and whirling round, he ...

"That's all?" asked Jed, looking up. "*All?*"

Melissa nodded.

Jed rubbed his forehead, as if he were now getting

the pre-flu headache. "Circlet," he muttered, studying the papers again. "Even the forest of winter curse. But — Melissa, if we only had the rest of it!"

"Jethro Ellison," ordered Gran, appearing with the teapot, two mugs, and an enormous plate of warm tollhouse cookies. "Kindly go straight back to the doorway where you belong! Your father will never forgive me if you catch this terrible flu!"

"He wouldn't even notice," Jed grumbled, but he went obediently back to the chair Gran had put at the threshold for him. "Anyway, about half my class has it already."

"It's this terrible weather," said Gran, taking a cookie herself after passing the plate to Jed and Melissa. "We're almost out of oil for the furnace, and the woodpile's low again — heaven knows what the village will do if there's another blizzard. I don't see how it can go on much longer — but I said that a month ago, and it did."

Melissa and Jed exchanged a glance, but neither of them said anything.

"Well," said Gran, "back to work. *I* know it's time for spring cleaning, even if the weather doesn't. Have a nice visit, you two, but really, Jed, please stay in the doorway. I'd hate for you to get this thing."

"You *would* hate it," Melissa said when Gran had left. "It's really rotten."

"How do you feel now?" Jed asked absently. He had put his mug down and was looking at Melissa's transcription of the cipher pages again, frowning.

"A lot better. Except my head still hurts sometimes."

135

"Do you think," he asked, looking up, "you'll be well enough next week to go up to the woods again?"

"To — to the hermit's, you mean?" Melissa asked slowly, though she knew perfectly well what he meant.

Jed nodded, then studied her face as if he were trying to read her thoughts. "We've got to give it another try, anyhow," he said with elaborate casualness. "We *know* something's going on now, even if" — he waved the cipher pages — "even if we still can't figure out quite what. Melissa — that thing about returning — " He shivered. "Did it get to you, too?"

Melissa nodded. "It doesn't *scare* me, though," she said, determined that it wasn't going to. But she knew that she was trying to convince herself as much as Jed. Then, as if the words had awakened another, braver Melissa inside her, she heard herself say slowly, "Gran said I could get up for a while tomorrow. I don't know when she'll let me go out."

Jed grinned. "How about school Monday and the woods Tuesday?" he suggested. "Or Wednesday. Meanwhile — well, you get my vote for first-class cipher cracker, even if you aren't a spy!"

Melissa felt her mouth smile at him, at the compliment, anyway.

But under the smile she felt her dread growing again. How was it Eben had put it? ". . . this premonition of Evill . . ."

On the following Tuesday, Gran did let Melissa go back to school, but it wasn't until Thursday that she let her stay outside in the afternoon with Jed.

Melissa was just as glad, though she could see that Jed was disappointed and impatient.

She lay awake most of Wednesday night staring into the darkness of her room, feeling its cozy familiarity all around her, wanting to snuggle so deep into the covers and the warmth that no one would ever find her, wanting to build herself a safe and sheltering nest as impenetrable as the armor she had built after her mother's death — but comforting instead of confining — a cocoon, perhaps, instead of armor.

But she forced herself up out of bed and, shivering even with her flannel bathrobe close around her, went to her side window and looked out.

The moon was high and cold, making deep-blue shadows on the pale-blue snow — snow on the ground, on her windowsill, on Gran's fence, on tree branches — branches close to the ground, on trees shrunk dwarf-short because the snow was so deep. And it was now a week into April . . .

A shadow moved; Melissa blinked, sure at first the wind was blowing, making a bush, and hence its shadow, move.

But it was not the shadow of a bush, or even a shadow at all. It was Ulfin, the moonlight turning his pale-gold coat nearly to silver, looking up at Melissa where she stood shivering at her window. He was wagging his tail slowly, invitingly, insistently . . .

The next day he trotted up to them, eyes bright and friendly, as soon as they'd climbed over Gran's wall and entered the woods.

He nuzzled Jed quickly and then jumped up on Melissa, his paws near her shoulders, and gave her face a long, slow lick as if to reassure her. When she stooped to pat him, he leaned against her, shaking his head slightly so that his tag jangled against his collar. He wouldn't stop till she had taken the tag reluctantly in her hand, decorated side up.

It wasn't that she didn't know perfectly well what she was going to find, what he was trying to show her. It was that she didn't want to find it, didn't want to have one more puzzle piece fitting a picture she couldn't yet quite see.

But by now Jed was kneeling beside her, looking at the tag himself.

"Look," he said softly, holding it out.

$$\triangledown \; \boxdot \times \; \approx \curlyvee$$

"U-L-F-I-N," she spelled out reluctantly, the dread growing stronger. "I know. It's the same cipher. Oh, Jed . . ."

Ulfin stood quietly while Jed examined the letters more closely. "I wonder how old this collar is," he said when he stood up again, after giving Ulfin a quick hug.

I wonder how old Ulfin is, Melissa almost said, but she dismissed it as another absurdity. At the very most, he was probably just descended from the Ulfin in the diary. If so many people in Fours Crossing had seventeenth- and eighteenth-century ancestors, why not the dogs, too?

"Okay," Jed said, ruffling Ulfin's ears. "Let's go, boy. You know what you want us to do — go on. We'll follow you."

Ulfin gave one sharp bark and ran ahead into the forest, bounding in and out of the fresh snow that covered their old tracks and stopping every once in a while to let Jed and Melissa catch up. As they approached the hermit's clearing he slowed, and then he stopped just before they came out into the open.

Melissa heard the hermit before she saw him. He seemed happy today, gleefully chanting at his tripod, an eerily exultant laugh rippling under every strange, foreign-sounding word. Held high in his hands, gleaming in the dim sunlight, was the fourth plate. The chant rose to a triumphant crescendo; Melissa could feel Ulfin trembling beside her, and when she put her hand on his neck, she felt something rumbling there — whether growl or whine, she couldn't tell.

The hermit stood motionless in the clearing, the plate still held high. Then slowly, silently, he lowered it over the tripod, balancing it on the place where the three sticks met and were fastened together. He turned abruptly then and went into the house.

There was silence in the clearing.

"We could grab it," Jed whispered, his eyes on the plate. "Before he comes out of the house again, we could just run into the clearing, grab it, and run home. It would be over then, I bet. We wouldn't even have to know any more . . ."

Over! Melissa heard nothing beyond that. Over — that was all she wanted. She bent her knees, ready to run . . .

Instantly Ulfin leaped in front of her, barring her

way and growling softly. He wagged his tail the moment she caught herself mid-step and stopped.

The hermit came out of his house again.

Melissa took Ulfin's face between her hands. "Thank you," she whispered, trembling; she'd almost run right into the hermit's arms!

Ulfin licked her face with infinite gentleness.

"Look," whispered Jed. "Melissa, look at him! He's got the robe on — oh, holy cow!"

Melissa, locking one arm firmly around Ulfin's neck, looked once again into the clearing.

The hermit had put on the white robe she and Jed had seen in the oak chest in his house; he had girded his waist with the golden chain that matched Ulfin's collar. Arms stretched out horizontally, he was slowly circling the tripod, chanting again but more quietly, almost mournfully, like an ancient bard or pagan priest. Circling — circling quickly — faster — faster — and his voice rose — and the wind came up — and the snow fell, covering Ulfin's coat and Jed's and Melissa's dark winter clothes, camouflaging them in white until they were three snow creatures frozen at the edge of the clearing, fascinated, hypnotized, as birds are before a snake.

The hermit whirled in a blurry flash of white; he was running now, nearly flying around the tripod, his robe billowing behind him. Or was that the snow, falling so much faster now that the hermit almost disappeared behind it? Melissa wasn't sure — until suddenly she was conscious of an absence of motion, as if, abruptly, he had stopped. For a moment she thought she saw him, standing ice-statue-still, his head bowed, near the tripod, a denser whiteness in the wildly whirling snow.

But then the whiteness seemed to diminish, and she sensed that he was gone.

Ulfin shook the snow off his coat and nudged first Melissa and then Jed away from the clearing.

They followed him silently through the forest in the snowstorm, back to Gran's.

everal times a week for the rest of that cold
and snowbound April, Melissa and Jed trudged
with Ulfin through the woods to the hermit's
clearing. Each day there was a little less oil in
Fours Crossing fuel tanks, and a little more trouble
getting deliveries through. More and more people
borrowed staples — flour, canned vegetables, sugar
— from neighbors — "Just till Mr. Titus gets more
in," they said, trying to smile. The ski train had long
since stopped running, because the calendar said
spring had come and the season was over — but
most days there was still too much snow on the
tracks for the railroad's snow train to clear it for
the freight that was supposed to run all year round.
Trucks did fare better, but most of the time only if
they had their own plows. Once, as Melissa and
Jed tramped through the woods, they found two

dead birds in the snow, and another time Melissa noticed a group of thin rabbits watching them from the edge of one of the hemlock tents, their round eyes liquid with hunger. From then on, Melissa carried cracked corn into the woods whenever she could, and scattered it for the wild creatures as she walked.

Time after time, they found the hermit at home, usually chanting incomprehensibly from inside the house, or sitting in front of it polishing the plate and muttering; once or twice they saw him cutting wood. Then one gray morning when the hermit was not outside and no smoke or sound came from his house, Melissa and Jed crept slowly forward, hearts hammering, ignoring Ulfin, who pranced in circles around them and growled. At last Ulfin gave Melissa's jacket a sharp nip — and she pulled Jed out of sight just as the hermit peered out of his door and shouted with angry clarity:

"Them! It's them again! Stay away, you hear? I want no part of you now!"

"He saw us!" Melissa whispered in horror when they had safely left the clearing. "Oh, Jed, what are we going to do now?"

"Go on," Jed answered grimly. "We can't do anything else."

But it was harder from then on.

On the first of May, Melissa went to school with a bunch of forsythia branches that Gran had cut in honor of the day. "Buds are still winter tight," Gran said sadly when she handed the thin branches to Melissa, "but maybe the warmth inside your classroom will open them. It's always nice to have something blooming on May Day."

"Oh, great," said Jed sarcastically when Melissa showed him the forsythia in the hall before the first bell. "Terrific. You don't think those buds are actually going to open, do you?"

Melissa touched one softly with her fingertip. "No," she admitted. "But it's nice to think they might."

Everyone in school seemed equally miserable, even though some of the pupils and most of the teachers had put on new spring clothes. Melissa had tied her hair back with a light-green ribbon, and even Jed was wearing a bright-yellow shirt over his usual faded turtleneck. But no one's cheerful clothes could take away the gray sky outside or the smell of damp woolen coats, mittens, and scarves indoors.

Listlessly Melissa opened her history book for the day's first lesson, and dutifully she went to art afterward, and then tried to concentrate on English and later, science. But by afternoon her mind felt so fuzzy she finally allowed it to drift into daydreams —

— Until a few minutes before the last bell when the door burst open and Melissa looked up in surprise to see Ulfin, his brightly flecked eyes blazing across the room into hers.

As soon as she saw him, he wheeled and ran down the hall to Jed's classroom.

Blindly, as if pulled by a strong force from far outside herself, Melissa followed Ulfin down the hall. She heard Miss Laurent call, "Melissa! Melissa, the bell hasn't rung yet!" but she heard it only faintly, as if from a great distance in a dream.

Jed was already in the hall stabbing his arms into the sleeves of his jacket, his eyes on Ulfin, who was bounding soundlessly down the stairs. "Come on," he said unnecessarily. "He's fetching us. It must be important — it must be time."

Melissa had already pulled her coat out of the girls' closet. She ran down the stairs after Jed, tugging it on.

Ulfin was waiting on the porch, no longer patient. His eyes still blazed like brittle fire, and he was panting, pawing the snow.

"Children!" Mrs.-Ellison-in-the-school-office called as they ran outside. "Where are you going? And whatever is wrong with that dog? Don't go near him," she shouted after Jed and Melissa. "He may be sick!"

Melissa and Jed barely heard her. They stopped only to strap on their snowshoes, ignoring Mr. Coffin, the postman, returning from his afternoon rounds, who looked, astonished, at his watch and then at them and the dog as they sped past.

Ulfin barked just once as they left the village, and then he dashed silently across the bridge, running up the hill faster than Jed and Melissa could follow. He glanced back at them impatiently before skirting around back of Gran's, and only at the near edge of the field did he finally wait for them to catch up — but even so, he was whining anxiously when they reached him, and he nudged them both sharply with his nose, urging them on.

When they came to the hermit's clearing, Ulfin stopped Jed and Melissa in his usual way and ran to the house alone. Then, after sniffing carefully around it, he pawed open the door and disappeared inside.

"He's checking," Melissa whispered, and Jed nodded. In a minute Ulfin was back, pushing them eagerly forward.

Ulfin stayed in the doorway alertly facing out when they went in, as if guarding them, watching for the hermit's return.

For of course the hermit wasn't there. A few coals glowed weakly in the big fireplace, but the iron pot was again empty, and there was little else to show anyone lived there — a few more dirty plates, perhaps, but that was all. The musty smell was if anything more pungent than before.

There was also no sign of the plate — though the tripod, Melissa had noticed as they'd scurried across the clearing, was still outside.

"Ulfin, where is it?" Melissa asked, going to him. "Where is it? You must know."

But Ulfin was acting almost like a normal dog again. He wagged his tail and licked Melissa's gloved hand with his big pink tongue — although he still kept his eyes on the forest.

"He's not going to tell us anything more, Jed," Melissa said, going back inside. "Maybe he doesn't know."

Jed was rummaging on the shelves. "Oh, yech," he said suddenly, almost dropping what he'd just picked up; then Melissa saw him put it aside gingerly.

146

It was a small pile of soggy, smelly animal skins.

Melissa turned away, telling herself that the hermit had to eat and that he was probably so poor he had to save the skins to make clothes or blankets, and that, at any rate, this was no time to be squeamish, which she usually wasn't anyway — and it was then that she saw the plate.

"Jed," she said, pointing.

There, buried under some ash-covered stones in the bottom of the fireplace, under the faintly glowing coals, was a quiet silver gleam.

Jed ran to the hearth and pushed aside the coals with his bare hands. The plate was buried more deeply than they thought at first, and all but one edge was carefully wedged under the stones, which fit cleverly together, like a false floor. Jed and Melissa dug so furiously to free the plate that Ulfin's warning bark registered on neither of their minds, and by the time they finally heard him snarl in fury and then yelp in pain, the hermit was already standing in the doorway, a great dark presence, blocking out the sun.

"So," the hermit growled, his black eyes snapping. "I catch you red-handed, isn't that the expression? I have seen you skulking around the edges of my house — but I know you, cleverly disguised as you are! And now I find you with your hands in my fireplace, trying to look as innocent as the children I know you are not — now what could you possibly be after, eh? A few soft breezes, a daffodil for you, my lady, and you, sir, a tulip for your buttonhole, h'm? They will be a long time coming . . ."

"Ulfin!" screamed Melissa as soon as she found

her voice. She pushed violently past the hermit, but he caught her hair as she reached the doorway and jerked her cruelly and quickly back.

Not so quickly that she didn't see Ulfin lying still on the snow outside.

Melissa saw Jed's fist swing out hard, but the hermit caught his arm before his blow could land.

"Oho," the hermit chortled nastily, his long white beard bobbing angrily as he talked, "you are stronger than you seem — I remember now! But I can still do something of my own, as you will learn; I am strong also. You wish to see the dog, do you? Well, as you should know, it was my dog once and it betrayed me, so I have punished it at last. It will be a traitor no more."

Melissa had little chance to wonder at the hermit's vague hints that he somehow knew them and that they understood more than they did, for he shoved them both roughly forward, maintaining such a grip on Melissa's hair that she had to keep her head bent back to stand the pain. "Have a look at how we punish traitors," the hermit said, holding them near the doorway. "Learn from it for yourselves. He will lie there till his body freezes, for I'll not bother to bury him, carrion that he is. To make sure . . ." The hermit shoved Melissa's head under his arm and picked up a rock that was lying just outside the door, but as he drew his arm back to throw it, Melissa stamped hard on his foot. He screamed, then dropped Jed's arm to seize Melissa's shoulders with both hands and shake her.

Quickly Jed ran toward Ulfin, but the hermit, first giving Melissa a violent push that sent her back into the house, got to Jed before he reached the dog. He dragged Jed back, shoving him into a far corner with Melissa, and then shut the door, bolted and barred it.

"So," he chortled, "I think that will be all the bravery for a while, eh? The traitor dog, as you can see, is dead, and I have" — he dug among the ashes and stones with his claw-like hands — "I have your springtime — the circlet, the sacred circlet-wheel has it. I have your daffodils, your soft breezes, your green leaves. How clever of them in the village to send you; I have always thought that. But this time . . ."

"But they didn't!" Melissa interrupted. "We came . . ."

The hermit cut her off, rubbing his hands together and chortling again. "You can tell them in the village — or you could if I let you go, which I shall not this time — you *could* tell them in the village that their world must remain cold and shining white to pay for their frivolity, their betrayal. This place must be made pure again, and until it is, there will be no bright reward of spring, no life."

Melissa looked at Jed, a glimmer of understanding beginning. "Circlet," Jed whispered, "the diary . . ."

"So," the hermit hissed softly, his whole manner now oozing lordly sarcasm, "so, my *lady*; so, my *fine* young gentleman." He bowed slightly to them, and an icy smile twitched at his lips, vanishing quickly but returning again as he sat down on a stool near the fireplace and began staring at them coldly.

Melissa's back ached, but she didn't dare move.

So this is my relative, she thought bitterly; this is who Gran was sorry for!

Since the hermit seemed inclined to remain silent, Melissa let her eyes slowly scan the room, looking for some way out, some way even just to see out to check on poor Ulfin — thinking of him made tears come close. But it was impossible to see, let alone to leave. There were only the cobwebby shuttered windows and the heavily barred door. The only real light in the room, since the fire was burned down to coals, came from a few candles in the rough pewter candle holders on the table.

Melissa cleared her throat; if they weren't going to be able to escape, they would have to talk their way out. "Um — you know," she began, ignoring Jed's warning glance, "you know, sir, I — we're relatives, you and I . . ."

The hermit turned his face toward hers, glowering coldly. "Oh, I know," he said, his voice thick with bitterness. "At least you claim it, marrying my son. But to me, Tabitha, you will never be aught but the Ellison you are — nor, Eben, will you," he said to Jed with great vehemence, "as long as you embrace not only the New Ways but a daughter of the New Ways as well."

"But . . ." Melissa began again, looking at Jed in panic, "but I'm — we're not . . ."

"And so," the hermit cried above her voice, as if in sudden pain, "I have had no son all this long time. There has been no follower, no successor, to carry on the Old . . . Aiiiiiiieeeee!"

While Melissa and Jed watched with growing horror, the hermit raised his arms above his head, his

150

sleeves flowing down like wings, and his agonized moan rose to a deafening shriek in the small room before it slowly, mercifully, died away into silence.

After a moment, he dropped his arms and seemed calm again. "This time," he said, getting up, his voice low now and intense, "this time you will not deceive me." He came toward them slowly, still speaking in the same low voice. "You will stay and you will learn, and this time — this time Eli Dunn will win!"

With a terrible laugh he lunged forward, seizing them each at the back of the neck. He pushed them into the other room, impatiently kicked open the door of the fireplace cupboard, and shoved them into the thick and musty darkness inside.

14

It was nearly six o'clock that night when Gran threw down her soup ladle, wiped her hands on her apron, and marched decisively down the hall to the telephone. "It's not like them, Pride and Joy," she said, moving the cat out of the way and then dialing. "Not like them at all."

"Fours Crossing Police," said a woman's voice, bored, after the phone had rung once.

"Sarah," said Gran, "I want to speak to Chief Dupres. It's Janet Dunn."

The woman's voice brightened; Fours Crossing was such a quiet little town that few calls were made to the police, and Sarah Goodel's job as dispatcher was seldom very exciting. "Why, hello there, Janet," she exclaimed. "How're you doing up there? Chief's home at supper now — can I help?"

"My granddaughter and Jethro Ellison ran out of school this afternoon with that strange dog that's been around," Gran said tersely. "No one's seen them since. Sarah — the chief, please!"

"Good Lord, Janet! Oh, my land — yes, of course, I'll ring the chief right away, quick's a lamb's tail — my Lord! You just hang on, Janet, hang on!"

There was a series of clicks, during which Gran realized she was twisting the phone cord into tangles.

"Mrs. Dunn? Chief Dupres here."

Gran quickly repeated the story.

The chief sounded calm when he spoke again, but his voice was very grave. "I'll be up right away," he said quietly. "As soon as I round up a man or two — mind you, I'm sure they'll turn up — probably just out skylarking, you know how kids are. But just in case . . . You sit tight now, don't you worry."

"Humph!" Gran snorted when the chief had hung up. She punched the button to break the connection and got a new dial tone. "Sit tight, indeed!" She consulted a long list of motel phone numbers and dates Melissa's father had sent her before he left on his trip, dialed one, and said, "Stanley Dunn, please," the moment there was an answer.

"Checked out two days ago," said a cold, impersonal voice. "No, no address or number. Sorry . . ."

Quickly Gran hung up and dialed the next number on her list, even though she knew her son wasn't due at that motel for several more days.

"No, ma'am, sorry. Yes, he did have a reservation here, but he just canceled it this morning."

Gran very nearly swore. Then, her lips pressed together in a thin, tight line that made her look nothing like her usual self, she went back into the kitchen. She turned off the simmering soup, fed Pride and Joy, and was just pulling on her boots when the police chief and two sergeants came stomping up the back steps, carrying huge flashlights, shovels, a hatchet, and an enormous coil of rope. "Just stash that stuff outside, Charley," Chief Dupres said, stepping between Gran and the man with the rope.

"What on earth . . .?" asked Gran, looking uneasily at all the equipment.

"Oh, just in case of emergencies — ice breaking on ponds, that kind of thing," said the man called Charley.

Gran sat down quickly at the table.

"No chance of that in this weather, anyway," said the chief cheerfully. He glanced casually around the kitchen. "Not back yet, I see?"

Gran shook her head.

"Well, well, we'll soon find 'em, don't you worry. Now, suppose you just give me a quick rundown as to what your granddaughter was wearing, Mrs. Dunn."

Gran answered his questions as calmly as she could. Then, after the men had disappeared into the woods, she went out to feed the chickens, telling herself that if she made the job last a long time the children would be back by the time she was through.

But they were not.

At seven-thirty-five, she took a flashlight and carefully searched the field herself for snowshoe tracks.

But it had snowed again; even the policemen's tracks were almost hidden.

Gran stood by the stone wall for a long time, looking deep into the forest, praying silently. But the woods remained empty, and she walked slowly home.

At eight-fifteen, Gran nailed a note for the police to her back door and struggled down the hill to Seth Ellison's cottage, though it was snowing harder now and a fierce cold wind was coming up.

There was no bluster any more in Jed's father when he came to the door and unsteadily let Gran in. "They say m'boy's missing," he whimpered, clutching her arm. "Gone . . ." He shook his head as if he didn't, couldn't, understand or even believe. "They say he's lost — lost . . ."

Gran took Seth's elbow and steered him through the cluttered living room to a tattered dark-red easy chair in front of the fire crackling in his open wood-burning stove. "Easy now, Seth," she said soothingly. "Easy now. You know how woods-smart that boy of yours is. He'll find his way back. I'm counting on it — my Melissa's gone, too, you know. Now, I'll just make you some coffee — perhaps if you drink it instead of that other stuff, you could even help look for them."

But even after downing two cups of Gran's strong black coffee, all Seth seemed capable of doing was staring at the fire, shaking his head, and muttering, "They say he's lost, but I dunno. I just dunno . . ."

Gran rinsed out the cup and the coffeepot and put on her coat, realizing it would be impossible to get Seth to think straight that night, let alone do anything helpful.

He followed her to the door and clutched her arm again. "You sure he's not run off?" he pleaded. "I — he might think he's got cause to."

"Yes," Gran couldn't help saying sharply then, "he *does* have cause. You've not given him much to come home to since Bethany died, Seth Ellison, and that's a fact. But, no, I don't think he's run off."

Even so, when Gran left, Seth was still shaking his head and muttering tearfully, "Run off — m'boy's run off."

Outside the hermit's house, and inside, too, there was thick, snow-wrapped silence. Night had long since fallen, and now the moon rose and started its slow trip across the sky, touching Ulfin's body with silver and, later, leaving it in shadow.

And then the shadow moved.

Slowly, painfully, the battered dog rose to his feet, his aching head heavy and low. He swayed a little, then steadied himself, and turned. With a valiant but unsteady attempt at the long, easy lope of his ancestors, he set off through the woods on a hidden path he had sometimes used for going secretly to the village. His aching head forced him to rest often, so it was not until dawn began to brighten the sky that he wearily climbed the steps of the school porch to escape the wind and the cruelly blowing snow. He found the leeside of the porch and curled up into as tight a ball as he could against the bitter cold and the emptiness in his stomach, warming his nose under his tail. There was nothing he could do until the People were up and out of their houses.

By breakfast time the next morning there was not a person in Fours Crossing who hadn't heard about the missing children — and that the hermit seemed to be missing, too, for that night the police had searched as far as his house and found him gone. "If you ask me," said Mr. Titus in the general store, pouring a cup of coffee for Frank Grange of the Highway Department, "and even if you don't, I bet that old codger's got 'em. I know some folks think he's harmless, but I allus said he'd turn bad. 'Tain't right, living all by himself like that in the middle of nowhere."

"Oh, I dunno, Alex," said Frank. "I never heard you say a thing against him till now. Funny how folks turn on other folks that's a bit strange soon's anything goes wrong. The old man allus seemed harmless to me."

"Well, you never know," Mr. Titus muttered darkly. "You joinin' that search party Henry Ellison's getting up?"

"Well, sure," said Frank Grange, gulping his coffee and reaching for his jacket. "Aren't you?"

Mr. Titus nodded.

Frank Grange left the general store just as Mrs.-

Ellison-from-the-school-office plodded dispiritedly up the school steps on her way to look for clues in Jed's and Melissa's desks. She lost her balance on a icy patch and tripped, waking Ulfin so suddenly he growled.

"Oh, my," Mrs. Ellison said, regaining her balance and then stepping back in alarm. "Oh, my!" She backed away slowly, keeping a wary eye on Ulfin, who by now was awake enough to realize she meant no harm and was wagging his tail to make amends for the growl. But Mrs. Ellison had fled down the steps and across the green to the fire station, where she knew she would probably find the dog officer having his morning coffee with the chief.

Ulfin lay down again, straight out and watchful, his head on his front paws.

A door slammed across the street; a voice called, "See you at lunch — mind you keep away from strangers," and a sixth-grader tiptoed by, a violin case in her hand, watchfully, as if she expected a kidnapper to pop out from behind a bush and snatch her away. Ulfin wagged his tail softly as she passed, but didn't lift his head or even shift his weight till Tommy Coffin walked soberly by with Tim and Joan. Tommy was too silent for Joan and Tim to dare speak, for his mind was far away in the woods at dawn on Spring Festival when Jed and Melissa had been so secretive and had run into the hermit's house when no one — except Tommy — was looking.

The moment Ulfin caught Tommy's scent, he bounded off the porch and plopped himself down in the path directly in front of him, holding up one paw as he had to Melissa that first day near Gran's mailbox.

Tommy looked as if he'd seen a ghost. "Why — why, it's that dog," he said slowly. "The one Jed says is his . . ."

Ulfin whined, and slowly Tommy reached out a hand to him.

"Careful," warned Tim. "My dad says when a stray acts tame it might have rabies."

"Oh, garbage," said Joan. "He's just being friendly. Nice doggie."

"What is it, boy?" Tommy asked softly. "What is it?"

The dog officer, with Mrs. Ellison trailing fearfully behind, tramped across the green and thrust the children aside. Ulfin, sensing danger, growled and laid his ears back.

"Hey, it's okay . . ." Tommy began.

"Move away," ordered the dog officer. "He may be dangerous."

Ulfin saw a quick movement behind the man's back and edged closer to Tommy. The dog officer, mistaking his move for a threat, pulled a net from behind his back and threw it with perfect aim over the dog before Tommy had a chance to jump between them or catch the net. Ulfin went down in a tangle of paws and legs and wildly thrashing tail. "NO!" Tommy shouted — but it was too late.

"Oh!" gasped Joan. "But I don't think he'd hurt anyone. Really — he's okay. I've seen him around."

"So have I," said Tommy angrily, tugging at the net. "You can let him go, he's . . ."

"Watch out, son," said the dog officer, pushing Tommy's hand away. "Someone claims him within fourteen days, okay. If not — well, you kids don't have to be told."

Joan and Tim looked at each other in horror. "He's *Jed*'s," Tommy protested desperately as the dog officer beckoned to his assistant, who was pulling up in a truck. "He's Jed Ellison's dog. At least, Jed knows him."

The dog officer lifted Ulfin into the truck, slamming the door shut — but not quickly enough to cut off Ulfin's anguished howl. "I didn't know Jed Ellison had a dog," he said a little more gently. "But — well, I'll still have to hold him, son. I'll call Jed's father if you like."

"Oh, you don't understand," Tommy said, blinking back tears of frustration. "Mr. Ellison — well, he might not know about it. But he *is* Jed's dog, and — and . . ."

"And it's not fair," Joan said, stamping her foot, "it's not fair to take his dog away when he can't even come and get him or tell you about him or anything!"

"Maybe" — Tommy gulped, following the dog officer as he went around the side of his truck — "maybe the dog could help look for Jed."

The dog officer put his hands on Tommy's shoulders. "Look, son," he said, "the law's the law. There've been complaints about this dog as it is.

Now he's threatened someone. I've got to quarantine him, see if he develops rabies . . ."

"He didn't bite anyone," said Tim slowly, "did he? Isn't quarantine just for biting?"

"He's a stray," the dog officer said wearily. "Come on, kids. You want the dog out, you find him an owner, or find his real owner if he's got one, in fourteen days. You want him to help look for Jed, you talk to the police about it, and to Mr. Henry Ellison. Mr. Ellison's in the Selectmen's office right now, getting up a search party, but . . ."

The dog officer didn't see much point in finishing his sentence, for by then Tommy, Tim, and Joan were already sprinting across the green.

But when they burst into the Selectmen's office, the search party had already left.

The group that hurried up the hill to the woods from Fours Crossing that morning was very different from the one that had gone there six weeks earlier to cut the tree for Spring Festival. Everyone in it was grim and sober, hushed this time not by dawnlight but by fear of what they might find. Some of the men carried long poles with which they gently probed snowdrifts for bodies. No one talked except for Henry Ellison, and his only words were terse commands as he led the search party through the forest and, later, even up into the foothills of the mountains surrounding Fours Crossing.

But though search parties methodically covered every inch of woods, hand in hand so they wouldn't miss even the smallest clue, they found no sign of Melissa, Jed, or the hermit. It was as if all three had fallen off the edge of the earth — or had been buried deep beneath its snow.

15

Melissa tossed restlessly, moving in and out of dreams, longing to be any place but where she was — wherever that might be; there didn't seem to be any way of even guessing where the hermit had taken her and Jed, let alone any way of escaping. He had left them in the dark cupboard for only a few moments, and then had pushed his own way between them and tied strips of rough burlap over their eyes. Snarling, he propelled them outdoors. For what seemed like hours they struggled blindly through deep snow, climbing over drifts and tumbling down them again, mercilessly driven forward by the hermit's gnarled but steely hands.

At last, with no warning, Melissa and Jed felt their feet stumble out of snow and onto rock.

"Ouch!" Melissa cried involuntarily as the hermit ripped off first her blindfold and then Jed's.

Melissa rubbed her eyes, which were itching from the rough burlap. By the light of the candle the hermit had lit she could see that they were in what seemed to be a medium-sized cave made of closely fitting stone slabs. It was almost impossible to find an opening in any of the walls — and yet, Melissa reasoned, there has to be a door somewhere; we must have just come through one. Finally she spotted a section of wall in which the outline of one rock slab was a little sharper and squarer than the others, and under which was a damp spot — tracked-in snow, she decided; it must be. But even so, the slab seemed to have no handle, no visible way of being opened, at least not from the inside — and there had been no sound, Melissa realized, of a boulder's being rolled out of and back into place when they'd come in.

The hermit had put his candle into a twisted black candelabrum on a rickety table in one corner, and after lighting several more candles and adding them to the same holder, he turned to them with a crooked, faintly amused smile. "There is more in Fours Crossing than you suspect, eh?" he said, taking two loaves of crudely home-baked bread out of a burlap bag he had apparently brought with him and slapping them down onto the table.

(Which, Melissa thought, reviewing that comment in her mind now as she lay uncomfortably near Jed in one corner of the cave, means that we must still be somewhere near the village, even if we did walk through the woods for what seemed like miles.)

"Here we will stay," the hermit had said when the candles were sending their soft light over the cold gray stone. He took Gran's silver plate out of the bag also and placed it carefully on a rough stone shelf that projected out of the wall at one of the shorter ends of the cave. "The entrance door has been firm since the Old Times," he said, nodding toward what Melissa had decided was probably where they had come in. "And now only I know its secret. So you will stay here with me and work for the Return. We have plenty of stores," he went on, gesturing to wooden shelves on one long wall; they were piled high with winter squash, pumpkins, turnips, carrots in boxes of sand, and potatoes; above, onions and herbs hung in bunches from iron pegs driven into rock.

"The root cellar," Jed whispered hoarsely to Melissa as the hermit turned away from them to bend over a small firepit scooped out of the center of the floor, laying kindling there. Melissa thought of Gran's story the night of the blizzard — hadn't there been a root cellar in it, near where the Festival tree used to come from?

After the fire had burned for a while, the hermit gave them bread and half-charred pumpkin that he had roasted in the ashes. Jed, Melissa saw, managed to eat several pieces of both, but she found she wasn't hungry for dry bread, and the pumpkin looked so revolting she could barely bring herself to smell, let alone taste, it. After the hermit himself had eaten, he pointed to a huge heap of rags under the vegetable shelves and said, "Your bedding — stuff rags into these sacks and pile them over there." He pointed to a corner opposite the stone shelf where the plate lay, softly gleaming. "Make up your beds now, and sleep."

But how could anyone sleep? Melissa thought; she was stiff and sore from the hurried walk and from her improvised mattress almost as soon as she lay down. The smoky fire had by now died down to coals, and chill dampness crept inexorably into the cave and into Melissa's bones. She wondered if Jed was as miserable as she — as cold, as lonely, as scared — for what was the hermit going to do with them now that he had them? It was creepy, the way he kept calling them Tabitha and Eben — as if to him, she thought, trying to burrow deeper against the cold, they weren't themselves at all but instead were people who'd lived centuries ago . . .

If only they'd never read the diary — if only they'd never found it, or taken it, or gone back to the hermit's house — if only the plate had never been stolen . . .

. . . If only Mumma had never died and I'd never come to Fours Crossing, she thought, wondering if she would ever see Boston — or Daddy — again.

She tried to imagine herself back there now, in Boston, last winter — no, the winter before, when Mum had still been alive. Christmas, that would be the best time, with the sweet smell of evergreens in the house, the warmth of all the baking . . .

But it turned into last Christmas instead, a bitter lonely one, with Mum in the hospital and Daddy sitting silently in his chair, rocking, rocking — and then had come cold January — and then February — and then . . .

And then she heard herself cry out, and from somewhere in the dark cave the hermit snarled "SILENCE!" reminding her horribly of where she was. Melissa subsided into miserable shivers, trying to keep her eyes open so she would stay safely awake — but it was so dark she couldn't be sure if they were open or not. She touched the lids with her fingers, forcing them open — for anything, even the hermit's cave, would be better than going back to where she'd just been in her dream: in her mother's dark grave, trapped deep beneath the surface of the earth, with her father at the edge looking down at her, stretching out a hand she could not reach.

In a few minutes there was a rustling nearby, and then Jed was at her side, fumbling for her hand. "I wanted to wait till he was asleep again," he whispered. "Melissa — it'll be all right. We'll get away. We'll think of something — you'll see."

She gripped his hand wordlessly, fighting the tears that she knew wouldn't come anyway.

Jed reached up as gently as Gran and clumsily brushed back Melissa's hair. "Melissa," he whispered, "you'll see him again, Melissa, you will, I promise."

"Him?" Melissa managed to ask around the thick place in her throat.

"Your father," Jed whispered. "You just called for him. I guess you were asleep — but you said 'Daddy' a couple of times."

Suddenly consumed with embarrassment, Melissa moved away and tried to free her hand.

"No!" Jed whispered fiercely. "I won't let go." He held tightly to her hand and his words rushed out like water from behind a cracking dam. "You know you've hardly mentioned him since you came to Fours Crossing? You've hardly said a word about him or your mother, or Boston, or anything. I . . ." Jed slowed down, as if he'd begun to look for the right words. "Well — at first I sort of wondered if, you know, if you really liked them — your parents, I mean, especially your father."

"I *do*," said Melissa, forgetting to whisper. "I do like him. I love him."

But her father's tearstained face came back to her, and though it was all mixed up inside with her dream and her present fear, she knew with shame that Jed was at least partway right.

"Shh," whispered Jed, "shh, you'll wake the hermit." He released her hand, but then touched her arm lightly. "Look," he said awkwardly, "I didn't mean to say any of this now — Melissa, I'm sorry, it just came out! And — well, you did call 'Daddy' in your sleep." His voice dropped; Melissa had to strain to hear. "Melissa, sometimes, right after my mother died, my father would — drink — get drunk — and he'd hit me, and I'd run up to your gran's and she'd comfort me and wash my back and give me cocoa and let me spend the night. Your dad's different, but — well, I know he hasn't exactly been writing you long letters every day, and — well, it's *okay* for you to be mad at him — if you are, I mean." Jed paused; Melissa could feel his fingers absentmindedly pulling at a thread on her sleeve. "The thing is, Melissa," he went on, his voice even softer than before, "the thing is that it's funny you just called out for your father, because — well, I'd been thinking about Fours Crossing and when we'd ever see it again, or your gran — that sort of led to Dad, I guess. It hit me all of a sudden that my father must have felt just as — as lost as us maybe, when my mother died. I don't know, it's just that if I ever do see Dad again, I — well, I'm not sure I really exactly *hate* him, anyway. So the thing is, maybe you don't — you know." He paused again and then said, "Melissa, I never could talk to anyone like this. Not even to your gran. I — I wish you'd talk to me."

Melissa ached to say, "I wish I could, too," but even those words stuck in her throat and she thought, with envy this time, of Jed's ability to talk at least when his troubles got bad enough to boil over, as Gran had said. But it was as if all hers could do was simmer.

"Okay," Jed said sadly after a few minutes of silence. "I guess I understand." He took his hand away; her arm felt cold, even where his hand had been. "We should be thinking about getting out of here anyway. That's more important. And getting the plate back." Melissa felt Jed turn away, but then his voice came out of the pitch blackness once more. "Melissa, I'll never be able to say this when it isn't dark. Melissa, don't let whatever it is inside you just sit there and eat away at you, the way things eat away at — well, maybe at the hermit — till there's nothing left. Or maybe the way they eat away at my dad, or yours, I don't know. Don't let that happen to you, Melissa, please!"

The rag heap at the other end of the cave suddenly rustled and heaved. "SILENCE!" the hermit roared again; Jed had barely enough time to dive back onto his bed before the hermit had lit a candle and was towering over them, huge and terrible, snarling, "One more sound, once more you wake me, and I will shake you till your bones rattle!"

For a blissful second when she first woke up, Melissa forgot where she was. But then a harsh voice chanting made her open her eyes, and when she saw the hermit, she remembered everything in a horrible rush that made her wish desperately for sleep again.

It was still dark in the cave, or rather, it was not fully light. The hermit had rekindled the fire, whose smoke, Melissa could now see, rose to an inadequately small opening high up in the cave's rocky ceiling. He had also lit the candles in the black candelabrum, and in odd stone sconces that lined the rocky walls. The candle flames plus the flames of the fire painted the gray stone walls and the old reddish-brown wood of the table and vegetable shelves with warm, deceptively cozy light. Light played on the hermit's long white beard as he stood by the fire, carefully stirring something in an iron kettle that hung from a tripod like the one outside his house, only smaller.

Breakfast, thought Melissa, suddenly ravenous in spite of everything — till she started wondering what it was.

When the hermit turned away, going to the low stone shelf, Melissa looked over at Jed's rag heap to see if he was awake and found him winking at her, his finger up to his lips in the *shh* sign. As soon as he had her attention, he pointed high up on the short wall opposite the stone shelf, above where their beds were.

There, about seven or eight feet up, was a small open chink in the rocky wall — about eight inches long and framed by small stones carefully set in what looked like moss. Coming through the opening was a thin band of grayish light.

Jed grinned when Melissa nodded to him to show that she had seen. Then he threw off his rag covers, saying cheerfully, "What's for breakfast?"

Breakfast turned out to be now-stale bread and stewed pumpkin — the latter much better than its roasted counterpart of the night before, but still nothing that Melissa would choose to eat; she found herself longing for Gran's porridge in comparison. Still, it was filling and hot.

After breakfast, the hermit rubbed his gnarled hands together and gave them his oddly crooked smile. He seemed fairly friendly now, at least much more than he'd been the day before.

"So," said the hermit, actually smiling. "So. Since you are here — Tabitha — Eben — and since you will not be leaving — and since you, Eben, now will have to succeed me despite your betrayal and your lack of caring, it is time for us to begin. Tabitha, you must only watch, and that as little as possible, for you are not of this family or this sacred line. You may, however, do the polishing, though you understand that even that might not have been permitted . . ."

171

"I'm not Tabitha!" Melissa shouted angrily, re-acting to the only part of his words that she fully understood. "My name is Melissa Dunn, so I am too of your family, and that's Jed Ellison, and your name may be Eli Dunn, but Gran says you're Eli *John* Dunn, and anyway you're not someone from long ago, the way you seem to be pretending to be! You've kidnapped us" — she caught her breath at the word, realizing as she said it that it was true — "*kidnapped* us! Don't you know you'll be caught and sent to jail?"

"Melissa," Jed warned softly.

"You may call yourself what you will, my girl," the hermit said in quiet cold fury, his friendliness vanished as totally as the cave's entrance, "but you cannot deceive me again, nor can my son-who-has-been-no-son! I am who I am and who I have been, as well you know. You, girl, are sharp-tongued like all your sex, and if you do not curb that tongue, I will curb it for you." The hermit reached into the burlap bag he had brought from his house and thrust a messy jar of dreadfully foul-smelling polish, a rag, and the fourth silver plate into Melissa's unwilling hands.

"Sit there," he ordered, pointing to a spot near Melissa's rag heap, "and polish the spring circlet, the new year's wheel. You," he said to Jed, seizing him roughly by the arm, "you sit here." He plunked him down onto an ancient three-legged wooden stool. "Do not look at her or let her hear any more than she must. Study this till it is part of you, as it should have been from the first." He drew a yellowed piece of parchmenty paper from a thin niche under

172

the vegetable shelf and laid it carefully on the table in front of Jed.

Jed twisted his head around to face the hermit, frowning. "Eb dedne dloc . . ." he sounded out with great difficulty, holding up the paper and stumbling over the peculiar sounds. "What kind of language is that?"

"Do not let her hear you so clearly!" the hermit shrieked. "She is not of our line, we cannot trust her yet, wife of yours or no! Perhaps in time, or if there is need — but for now, she must be considered ordinary, not of the priesthood."

There was a sudden silence, as if all three of them had simultaneously forgotten to breathe.

"The *what*?" whispered Jed, and Melissa, clinging desperately to the little that seemed left of reality, sputtered, "What — what do you mean, your line? I'm a Dunn like you, I told you! He's the Ellison, he's not your . . ."

The hermit stopped her before she could say any more; he strode to her corner and grabbed her arm, shaking her till she cried out in pain. "I told you to curb your tongue! And I will shake you till your bones not only rattle but also break the next time you disturb me."

Jed had already leaped to his feet, but the hermit whirled and thrust him angrily back onto his stool. "You are so far from being ready to wear the robes, my son-who-has-been-no-son, that I wonder why I do not pickle you instead of taking such pains to teach you. But teach you I must, for the sake of the Ways — though I must tame you both first, like wild animals. You" — he shoved Melissa back into her corner — "tend to your polishing and block your ears. Sing — that's it — surely you know a song." He glowered at her, waiting.

Mellissa sang the first thing that came into her head:

> *The farmer in the dell,*
> *The farmer in the dell . . .*

And while she fought to control the impulse to laugh hysterically at the silly song she'd chosen and at the ridiculous trappings of their all-too-serious plight, and at her frustrating inability to return the insults with which she had just been heaped — as she sang, Jed's reluctant voice struggled again to pronounce the strange words from the paper the hermit had handed him:

> Eb dedne dloc sretniw
> Ew devas, gnirb srewolf
> Raeb gnivil ew eert gnivil
> Erar, revlis, telcric eurt morf . . .

As Jed read, corrected every once in a while by the hermit, who had taken the gleaming new gold-belted white robe from his bag and put it on, the thin gray light that shone through the chink high in the wall faded slowly and then vanished.

"Weird," muttered Frank Grange back in Fours Crossing, looking up at the sky as his battered front-end loader crunched into another snowdrift. "Could've sworn the sun was just about to come out — did you see that, Joe? All-of-a-sudden-like those old clouds rolled in again — like someone pushed 'em, almost. Weird!"

But Frank's fellow worker Joe was too weary to notice, for he'd been out most of the night with the Selectmen's search party. The last thing Joe wanted to see was yet another sign that this winter was never going to end.

16

That same morning Mr. Coffin, the postman, again got a shock as he passed the Fours Crossing school. It was only nine-thirty, but every child in the school was streaming out the front door and down the steps. Fire drill, Mr. Coffin said to himself at first — but no, the strange procession marched straight across the green toward the police station, with Tommy Coffin (who was the postman's grand-nephew) in the lead, his green cap askew and a large piece of rolled-up paper in his hand.

Not a single adult — not even Mrs.-Ellison-from-the-school-office — came outside to call the children back, so Mr. Coffin, after scratching his head and staring, decided it was none of his business and continued on his rounds.

The dog officer, however, making his way back across the street after his usual morning session with Miss Laurent's father, the first chief, couldn't ignore the procession the way Mr. Coffin had, for the long line of children marched straight around the side of the police station and arranged itself in a neat knot behind it, outside the door to the pound.

"We've come for the dog!" Tommy shouted as the dog officer pushed his way through the crowd. "For Ulfin."

Joan Savage stepped froward. "What he means is, we'll keep him for Jed till Jed's found. We know we have to get him out of the pound before fourteen days are up or — or — you know."

The dog officer was by now leaning against his door as if he welcomed its support. "Well, now," he said, rubbing his chin. "Well, now. I don't know as anything'd happen to that dog if he had to stay a little longer than usual. When," he asked gently, "was the last time you kids heard of anything bad happening to a dog in this pound, h'm?"

Tommy looked a little flustered, but he straightened his cap and thrust the rolled-up paper out to the dog officer. "Here," he said. "We all signed it."

The dog officer unrolled the paper:

WHEREAS [it began]
We the undersigned students of Fours Crossing School do not believe in the practice of putting lost dogs to sleep just because no one comes for them in fourteen days, and

WHEREAS

No one's found Jed yet and Ulfin can't help look for him if he's shut up in the pound, and

WHEREAS

Ulfin has shown no signs of rabies anyway, and

WHEREAS

Even if he doesn't exactly belong to Jed (like having a license) he is a friend of Jed's, and

WHEREAS

We the undersigned will take all responsibility for him,

WE HEREBY REQUEST

That Ulfin be released to us.

Joan, whose father was a lawyer and had helped them a little with the wording, had wanted to add FORTHWITH at the end, but Tommy and Tim had both thought that might be going too far.

Almost 150 names were at the bottom of the paper, some printed and some in script.

"Well, now," said the dog officer again.

Tommy held out two one-dollar bills and a handful of change. "Three dollars," he said. "For the license."

"I see," said the dog officer. "Whose — ah — whose name will you be licensing him in?"

"Jed's," Tim answered promptly.

"And who will — er — look after him? Feed him and take him to the vet when he's sick?"

"We're all going to take turns," said Tommy, "till Jed comes back. The Sevens and Eights, anyway."

"And," said Joan, not looking at Tommy, "if Jed

doesn't come back, we think Mrs. Dunn might keep him. We didn't ask her yet, but we think she would."

"I daresay," the dog officer replied. He looked gravely into Tommy's eyes. "What about the rabies law?" he asked. "You know an animal that might have rabies has to be watched for fourteen days. You know Mrs. Ellison said he was acting queer . . ."

"My father says that's only when an animal's bitten someone," Joan put in quickly. "That's what the law says. And," she added triumphantly, "Ulfin hasn't bitten anyone." She turned to the others. "Has he?"

There was a deafening chorus of no's.

The dog officer scratched his head. "Well," he began. He shifted his weight from his right foot to his left foot and back again. Then he cleared his throat, said, "Excuse me," and vanished around the corner into the police station.

"Now what?" Tim asked Tommy.

"I bet he's going to ask Chief Dupres," groaned Tommy. "Oh, Christmas."

The whole crowd waited in uneasy silence until the dog officer came back out.

"Well?" Tommy asked impatiently.

The dog officer looked at them sternly. "I want you to promise me two things," he said in a loud voice, as if he were making a speech. "One, that you'll keep a muzzle on Ulfin for the rest of the fourteen days. Police orders. And two, that no one — *no one* — will take him out to look for Jed and Melissa without an adult or without permission. If you don't agree, I can't release the dog."

"But . . ." began Joan. Then she shrugged and glanced at Tim, who shrugged and looked at Tommy.

"Where do we get a muzzle?" Tommy asked cautiously.

"I've got one in the office."

"Will it hurt him?"

The dog officer's face softened and he put his hand on Tommy's shoulder. "Tommy, I *like* dogs," he said. "My wife's allergic — that's why I'm dog officer, so I can be around them just the same. No, son, a muzzle won't hurt him. You'll have to keep him leashed as well as muzzled, but — well, a leash is better than a cage."

Tommy took a deep breath. "Well, but about the looking," he began.

"Right!" someone shouted from the crowd; and someone else said, "If we can't *look* — well, that was a big part . . ."

"Not without an adult," said the dog officer sternly, raising his voice again and sending it out over the crowd. "And not without permission. No wandering around up in the woods, either."

"But . . ." protested Joan again.

"Listen, kids," said the dog officer, "it's only sensible. Sure, the dog might be able to help — but on the other hand, search parties have gone over every inch of the woods and no one's found anything yet. You know what Chief Dupres did this morning? He called the New York State Police, the Vermont State Police, the Maine State Police, the Massachusetts State Police — he even called some police up in Canada . . ."

No one said a word.

"There's no telling what's going on up there in the woods," the dog officer went on. "We don't want any more kids disappearing — so you've got to promise."

Now there was a lot of impatient murmuring and nudging from the crowd, but Tommy still hesitated, frowning deeply and scratching under his cap as if he had a terrible itch. At last he said, "Okay. We won't look without permission." Then he asked, "If we get an adult to go with us, though, we can go, can't we? Up to the woods to look?"

"With police permission," said the dog officer firmly again. "No one's allowed up there now without that — not even grown-ups. Promise?"

Tommy looked at the others, and especially at Joan and Tim; they nodded. "Promise," he agreed reluctantly.

The dog officer grinned. "Come get your dog, then."

The cheer was so loud it made old Bradford Ellison's statue tremble on its base.

The only Canadian police Tommy had ever heard of were the Mounties — the Royal Canadian Mounted Police. He'd even dreamed someday of joining them, maybe with Jed, when he grew up — for in the books Tommy had read, the Mounties were always heroes; they always got their man. But that's in Canada, he reasoned, where they know the terrain. Down here — well, Fours Crossing is Fours Crossing, not the Northwest Territory or some place like that. And even though Fours Crossing is a lot tamer than the Northwest Territory, right now it is also — well, a lot less *normal*, was the way Tommy put it to himself. Ever since Jed and Melissa had first disappeared, Tommy's suspicion that something weird was going on had been growing, and by now he was certain of it. Whatever that something was, Tommy felt sure that it was not the kind of thing that ordinary matter-of-fact adults would be able to do anything about, because they probably wouldn't even see that it was happening — whatever it was. So if he and the other kids weren't going to be allowed to take Ulfin out into the woods by themselves, they'd have to find not just any adult but the right kind of adult to go with them. Tommy knew his own father wouldn't do — he was kind, and he knew his way around the woods as well as anyone, but he'd never been able to see much farther than his own backyard in his imagination. Besides, he'd said just last night that he was sure Jed and Melissa had gotten lost in the snow and — well, would never be found alive again. That's what Tommy's mother thought also, and even though she hadn't said anything, Tommy was sure Miss Laurent felt the same by now, deep down.

What we need, Tommy decided, is someone who hasn't looked before, and someone who'll want so much to believe Jed and Melissa are alive they won't bother about anything else.

That meant family, of course. Melissa's grandmother? Tommy was pretty sure Chief Dupres wouldn't agree to it, even if he himself was pretty sure Mrs. Dunn was just about as strong as any of them despite her age. Melissa's father? As far as Tommy knew, no one had been able to get in touch with him yet. That left . . .

Tommy dismissed his first reaction to that thought, assumed his most efficient, military posture, and marched briskly next door to Jed's house.

They were almost out of water, Melissa realized with alarm later that some morning, dipping a tin cup into the leather bucket that served them as a well. She glanced over at Jed, who was still at the table chanting; the hermit, in his soft white robe with the gold belt, was holding the plate high above the firepit tripod, chanting softly under Jed's chant, nodding in approval when Jed got the words right and frowning when he didn't.

Stop, she wanted to shout at them both — but instead she took a sip of the flat-tasting water and returned to her corner, trying not to remember what she'd read about the short time — three days, wasn't it? — that human beings could live without water. And it's not only water for drinking we want, she thought, running her fingers through her dirty, tangled hair and discovering she had lost the spring-green hair ribbon she had put on with such optimism only the day before. What about a bath? Even just a face wash.

Melissa glanced up at the chink Jed had pointed out to her earlier; was it her imagination or had a snowflake just fallen through and landed on her cheek? It was hard to tell; she was already so cold and damp one snowflake was hard to feel.

And it's gotten colder and damper since Jed's

been chanting, she thought, not wanting to acknowledge it.

"Good," said the hermit, as Jed recited "Eb dedne dloc sretniw" for maybe the sixth time. The hermit lowered the plate to the point of the tripod, and then stood still for a moment, head bowed, apparently exhausted. "Good. It is done for now." He looked at Jed with something akin to affection. "You are doing well, my almost-son," he said, smiling.

Melissa turned away; it was in many ways better when he yelled at them — she trusted him more then.

The hermit removed his white robe, folding it carefully and laying it reverently down on a shelf next to but not touching the pale orangy-tan winter squash. He then unfolded his everyday black cloak, settled it over and around the dirty, skin-like shirt and breeches he wore underneath, and picked up the nearly empty water bucket. "Take the circlet," he instructed Melissa, "and polish it till I return. We are in need of water, as" — he looked with disconcerting perception at Melissa — "as I think you have discovered. The circlet, Tabitha."

Uneasily, Melissa got up and took the plate off the tripod, returning with it to her corner.

"You, Eben," the hermit went on. "You hesitated in the eleventh line, and you missed a word in the thirteenth. The eighteenth you reversed with the nineteenth. I will hear you say the chant perfectly when I return." His voice deepened suddenly, making both Jed and Melissa look up. *"Hear me!"* he boomed. "I am your teacher, your priest, and a prophet. I am already aware that the moment after I leave you will wish to scurry outside, like two trapped squirrels. And I am already aware that you will watch me in my leaving to discover the secret of the door. So I will tell you now that there are secrets from deep in the Old Times that you will never learn — and — this — is — one!" With those words the hermit raised his arms over his head and whirled three times, moving as he whirled to the entranceway, his black cloak billowing around him and blurring the outline of his body as well as briefly hiding the wall — and then he was gone.

Melissa blinked and rubbed her eyes.

"Holy cow!" said Jed, getting up cautiously. "That door thing isn't even open!"

Melissa went quickly to the wall. "But it *was*," she said. "Look." She pointed to a thin line of melting snow along one section of the bottom.

Jed put his shoulder to the wall, where they could now see that a slight indentation really did form the rough outline of a low door in the rocks, as Melissa had suspected. "I can't budge it," he gasped, his face very red.

"Maybe there's a secret catch," Melissa said, and they both felt carefully along the wall.

But they found nothing.

"Well," said Jed briskly, "we've just got to find another way out. He said we wouldn't be able to find this one — but he didn't say anything about not finding another." He glanced dubiously up at the smoke hole.

"Too small," Melissa said, "even if we could reach it. But . . ." She dragged the table and then Jed's three-legged stool to the wall where the chink showed. She put the stool on the table and looked around for some way to brace it, so she could climb up on it.

Jed's eyes darted around the cave. "Maybe we could use this for a shovel," he said, pulling a small rectangular tray out from under a heap of squash. The tray was a silvery metal, badly tarnished except for where the squash had been piled on it. But it was bright where it had been protected from the air.

"At least," Jed went on, turning the tray against his knee and trying to bend it, as if to test its strength, "maybe we could use it as a sort of crowbar to pry out those stones."

Just then a ray of renewed light from the chink in the wall glinted off the untarnished part of the tray, catching Melissa's eyes. And then she gasped.

"Jed," she said in a hushed whisper, staring in a direct line from the tray to the wall above the rough stone shelf opposite the chink.

There, deep in the wall above the shelf was the faint but distinctly glittering outline of a plate just like the one the hermit called the circlet.

But the plate itself was lying on the floor, where Melissa had dropped it when the hermit had disappeared.

Tommy had expected surliness from Seth Ellison; he had even expected to have to dodge a drunken blow or two. But he hadn't expected what he found when, after no one answered his knock, he walked into Seth's small living room.

Seth was sitting in has tattered chair, his eyes empty-looking and red, a bottle on the table beside him. He was as still as a dead man, as if he had no awareness that someone else was in the room with him.

"Mr. Ellison?" Tommy said softly. "Mr. Ellison? It's Tommy from next door. I've come about Jed. Mr. Ellison?"

But Seth still sat there, not moving.

Tommy didn't know what to do. Was Jed's father sick? Should he get Dr. Ellison? The police, maybe? He reached out a tentative hand and touched Seth Ellison's arm.

"Mr. Ellison?" he said again, and then he shouted it: "MR. ELLISON!"

Very slowly, so slowly it was hardly a motion at first, Seth turned his head. He blinked several times and ran his hand over his eyes. Then at last he said, "Hello, Tom," very softly. "Jed isn't here, you know." He sounded far away, but almost sober, despite the bottle nearby.

Tommy nodded, too unsure of Seth's mood to speak just yet.

Seth sighed deeply and took a long swallow from the bottle.

"Do — would you like a glass?" Tommy asked finally. Then he blushed. What a dumb thing to say! But he felt he had to say something before he told about Ulfin, and that was the first thing that came to him.

Seth laughed shortly. "It has the same effect, glass or no. And there's no glass clean."

Wordlessly, Tommy picked a dirty glass up off the floor, took it into the kitchen and washed it, and then set it down beside Seth. He was sure that was what Jed would have done, and the more Seth thought about Jed right now, Tommy guessed, the better.

Seth held the glass to the light, gazing through it into the fire. "Cleaner'n Jed would've washed it," he said as if to himself. "More like my Bethany's work. Jed — he washes stuff any which way, never gets anything clean."

Tommy took a deep breath. "Well, it must be kind of hard to do all the washing and the cleaning and the cooking and stuff and go to school, too. I mean . . ."

"Right," Seth replied calmly. He put the glass down and looked searchingly at Tommy. "I expect that's why he's run off, don't you? I don't suppose you know where he is, do you?" He peered closely at Tommy. "Well? Do you?"

"Oh — oh, *no,*" Tommy said emphatically. "I don't know where he is but I'm sure he hasn't run off. No one thinks he has . . ."

"Come on, boy, I haven't been sitting here all this time thinking about it for nothing! Drunk or sober, the thought's the same: he's run off. I don't give him much to come home to, Miz Dunn said. Well, busybody or not, she's right. And I've decided to let him go . . ."

Tommy brushed a sock off a small hassock and

pulled the hassock up to Seth's chair. "Some people in the village are saying that the hermit's got them," he said slowly, to make sure Seth followed. "That he's taken them some place. Um — kidnapped them."

Seth's chair creaked as Seth turned in it, interest kindling in his eyes at last.

"Look," Tommy went on, "I — I don't know where Jed is, honest. But there's this dog — maybe you've seen him — a sort of stray who used to hang around Jed. Mr. Ellison, I've got the dog — Ulfin's his name — he keeps pulling me up to the woods. I know it sounds silly but he might know where Jed is. But — but the police won't let anyone go up there without permission, and they won't let us kids go without an adult. Otherwise I wouldn't bother you. But — well, I thought you might . . ."

Seth leaned back in his chair; he closed his eyes and Tommy saw a tight muscle twitch at one corner of his jaw.

"Jed doesn't — doesn't dislike you, sir," Tommy said in a low voice, trying to guess what was holding Seth back. "Really, he doesn't. Not deep down."

Seth shook his head and reached again for the bottle.

Tommy waited, but this time Seth remained silent.

Finally Tommy stood up. "I — I've got the dog, sir, like I said. And I'd like to take him up to the woods to look some more. I know my dad won't go because he's already said he's sure himself they're — um — not there. Mrs. Dunn, she'd go, but no one would let her, I think." It was harder for Tommy

189

to say the next thing because part of him wished it weren't true. But he went ahead and said it anyway. "Jed would come home to you, sir, if he could, and if he knew you wanted him to."

Seth filled his mouth, swallowed, and still said nothing.

"Would you — just think about it?"

The fire crackled and a log broke. Tommy heard a sleigh go by in the snow outside, and then heard his mother's voice from next door, calling him home. Outside, where Tommy had tied him by Seth's door, Ulfin gave a single impatient bark.

"I'll be back," Tommy said. "Okay? I've got to go now, but I'll come back — and cook you some food, maybe, and maybe clean the place up — like Jed would. Okay?"

Seth didn't say yes, and he didn't nod. But he didn't say no either.

17

The man who stopped his car for old time's sake at the Fours Crossing depot late the same afternoon was a little stooped but far from old, even though his hair was gray and his pale face was deeply lined. The elderly conductor, who worked as freight dispatcher in the off-season, came out of the station to explain to whoever it was that nothing but freight, when it could get through, would move on the track till next ski season. Then he saw who the man was, tipped his hat, and said quietly, "Mr. Dunn — what a sad business. I mind bringing her here just about ten weeks ago. Quiet little thing — shy, I'd say. Polite and grown-up, like — pretty, too. I hope you find her, sir."

"Thank you," the man said, tipping his hat as the conductor went sadly back inside.

Stanley Dunn — for of course the man was Melissa's father — looked as if he was struggling with more than memories as he gazed toward the little village of Fours Crossing from the railroad station. It hadn't changed at all since the last time he'd been there with Melissa and Margaret, his wife, for a visit — years ago, that had been. The only difference now was the amount of snow — more than he'd ever seen — and he shivered involuntarily, thinking of what his mother had said when he'd called her that morning from Massachusetts — that Melissa was lost out there some place in the wild northern New Hampshire woods — lost just when he'd decided to cut his trip short and come home to her.

Capable little Melissa, he said to himself miserably. I was so full of my own sorrow I forgot you've only thirteen years behind you . . .

Melissa held up the metal tray, turning it at various angles to the light, experimenting. There seemed to be only one way to make it bounce enough light off the wall so that the deeply embedded outline became visible.

"It's awfully well hidden," Jed was saying, examining the bits of silver and mica so skillfully carved and set into the wall that they were invisible till light struck them at just the right angle. There were even hints within the outline of the leaf decorations, the cipher letters for "springe" and the L-shaped quarter of the cross.

As Jed was pointing that out, the hermit entered, so softly they heard nothing till they heard his voice.

Growling wordlessly, his black eyes flashing, he dropped his bucket of snow and snatched the tray from Melissa. He held it as she had and saw what she had seen. It was clear, from the way he threw the tray down then and glared at them, that he had not only seen the embedded plate before but that he had also considered it safely hidden.

While Jed and Melissa huddled together near the shelf, not daring to move or speak, the hermit paced restlessly, sometimes glancing up at them, but most of the time looking at the floor and muttering. Then at last he faced them, sighing in what seemed to be resignation. "You have seen," he said softly, "a great secret, prematurely and by accident. I had not intended to start that part of the teaching now; it is much too soon. But you have seen, so you must be told. Eben, you would have learned in time. You, Tabitha" — he whirled on Melissa angrily — "because you are not of our line, you should not have known. I shall truly have to make you a priestess now, in protection — a temple priestess, serving the circlet and never leaving . . ."

Temple, thought Melissa, trying to remember the diary — but the hermit gave her no time to think. "Sit," he ordered briskly, "at the fire. Eben, make us warm."

Knowing that she had no choice, Melissa sat and watched as Jed obediently brought more wood and piled it on the fire till smoke rose and the flames grew again. An eerie silence suffused the cave; the hidden outline, now that the tray was on the floor, was no longer visible — it might not be there at all,

193

Melissa thought, staring at the spot, which was now as blank and rough as all the other walls.

"Yes," said the hermit, following her eyes, "they were clever, the Ancestors; we were clever." He turned to Jed. "Our line are teachers, priests, if you will," he said simply, his anger apparently gone again. He spoke, in fact, with reverence and, gradually, with a kind of wonder that began to affect Melissa the more she realized it was her family he was talking about, not Jed's; in the hermit's eyes was a peaceful light Melissa had never seen there before.

"We are Guardians of the Old Ways," he said with an almost gentle smile, "Wise Ones. Do not be sure, you who are still young, that everything that ever happened has been written in a book and found its way into a school. There is more lore and more history than most know. I tell you what was told me and what I have lived; you may believe or not, as you choose. Most, of course, choose not to believe, but" — and here his gentle manner faded and the old harsh glint crept back in his eyes — "but follow it you must, whether you believe or no, for you are here and you have seen and you will not be permitted to return to the village and bring traitors here to — to desecrate the temple . . ."

The hermit lapsed into silence, gazing into the fire. Melissa looked over at Jed to see if he shared her thoughts — but he shook his head; she agreed it would be better not to move or speak. And so they sat.

In a while the hermit stirred the fire, making the flames leap up again, and he held his hands out as if to warm them. Melissa saw again how old his hands looked — dry and twisted, the bones showing sharply through the brittle skin, skeleton-like despite their strength, as if . . .

She shivered.

"The temple?" Jed prompted.

"In good time," answered the hermit, and he again sat in silence, frowning, for so long that Melissa was afraid he had fallen asleep and that she would, too, if somebody didn't say something soon.

"Long ago," the hermit said, just as Melissa's eyes closed, his lips barely moving and his voice coming from so deep inside him it sounded far away, "long, long ago, our small — band — came here to this northern place and lived quietly, farming and following the Ways. For a while all was peaceful. There was the village for living in, the woods and sawmill for supplying warmth and timber, the fields that we cleared for the crops and beasts; we had good mountain water and" — he waved his hand around the cave — "this temple, facing east for the spring dawn, for the starting of the year. The ignorant" — he smile — "have called it a root cellar. And root cellar it has been, when there was need — as you see, it can serve that purpose, though it is too damp for some crops. But no matter how disguised, it was and is and will forever remain a temple."

Melissa felt a chill greater than that inside the cave. In the long silence that followed, one of her feet grew numb and she shifted position slowly, trying to ease it without the hermit's noticing. But he saw.

"When you have been priestess for a time, girl," he said without anger, "you will be able to sit for days with no motion."

Melissa shuddered, and the hermit went on.

"At first," he said, "and for a while, the Old Ways were followed in Fours Crossing, under Eli Dunn, the leader. That is I." He blinked, his madness — for he must be mad, insane, Melissa told herself, if he's real at all — his madness seemed to deepen.

"The Ceremonies," he continued, "were followed then without omission, with deep and solemn joy, as befits them."

"Spring Festival," Jed murmured. "The tree . . ."

The hermit smiled in straightforward approval. "You are correct," he said, "and I welcome my son again. Yes, what is now called Spring Festival and demeaned with incompleteness and altered, weakened words — foolish jollity instead of deep, pure joy. But the Old Ways, of course, are strong enough to withstand such sacrilege, though I fear — I know — they weaken." Now the hermit's eyes snapped angrily. "The insult!" he said, his voice catching with the words. "The endless insult to so shatter the true Ceremony!"

"What is the true Ceremony?" Jed asked softly when the hermit seemed about to lapse into silence again.

"The true Ceremony," answered the hermit after a moment, "is this. The tree is cut from the pine grove at night, not morning, as is done now out of laziness. It is held for the balance of the night opposite the temple's eastern door." He pointed to the

196

chink high in the wall behind them. "And at dawn
— oh, moment of glory! — the equinoctial sun as
it rises shines through the branches at the top of the
tree and onto the true circlet above the altar — as
you accidentally saw, at least somewhat, with the aid
of that traitorous tray. The shadow of the tree falls
on the true circlet, and the light of the true circlet
falls on the tree, so there is endless communion between them, and when the tree is borne in procession
back to the village, it has spring's light upon it. That
light is taken to the base circlet — the one you so
foolishly call a plate — in the village, and when it
has also received that first light, spring returns to
the village and the year begins."

Melissa felt herself shiver once more, but not with
cold. The hermit fell silent again, and they all three
sat quietly, watching the fire but without seeing it.
". . . *a way of 'taking' spring,*" the folklore book
had said, "*believed to arrive first in one certain sacred place, to another place . . .*" Melissa looked at
Jed, who was still staring into the flames; surely it
was this simple story that someone had rudely ripped
from the Fours Crossing history book, as if it were
somehow evil. But how could it be evil? It was a
beautiful story . . .

But a story nonetheless.

Wasn't it?

"Why," Jed asked very softly, "did you take the —
base circlet from the village?"

"Because," said the hermit, his voice rising again
and his eyes snapping, "because when that — that
beast, your father, Tabitha — when that Ellison who

called himself priest came here to cast out the Old Ways and set his daughter to bewitch you, my son, the Old Ways began to weaken and to die. Oh, the year still began; the Ways are too strong to be broken altogether by unbelievers. But they weaken — they weaken sadly when they are not revered. And" — he leaned with great ferocity across to Jed; Melissa saw Jed shrink back in sudden bewildered fear — "and you betrayed me, you and your wife, coming out to my lonely house with soft words and the pale dog you took from my dog's litter — you remember; why do you think I forget? And then in the end your same traitor dog led you and the villagers to me, trapping me in my own temple — have you truly no memory? — stealing . . ." The hermit stood abruptly; the firelight made reddish gleams on his hands and his beard, and set shadows to dancing on his cloak. ". . . stealing at the last — oh, base betrayal — the year, the spring, the sacred rite!"

The hermit raised his arms; Jed's face, Melissa saw, had suddenly gone very white. She reached out to touch his hand, but it was cold and leaden, as if he had forgotten she was there, so she pulled her own hand quietly back. The end of the diary, she kept thinking; the stony floor, old Eli was — what had Eben written? ". . . *some Prehistoric Worme, some mythic Dragon, some Phoenix born of Death . . . I will return*" . . . She shrank from the hermit's gaze, full on her.

"And so, yes, I have taken spring," the hermit said, his arms still above his head. "I have taken spring *back*. And I will keep it until the traitor villagers are gone from this sacred place, and the place and you are purified. Only then will I allow spring to come — only when the Old Ways will no more be mocked. I will do this — and this time you will help me . . ." The hermit broke off suddenly and sat again by the fire, motionless, as if in a trance.

Jed beckoned to Melissa, and they crept away to their sleeping corner.

"It — it *can't* be true," Melissa said, shaking her head. "It can't! It's not possible for him to be . . ." She abruptly switched her thoughts to more plausible ones. "It's just that he's crazy. He's read it himself, the diary, and he's — he's acting it out."

"True or not, and acting or not," Jed whispered grimly, "it all seems to be happening again, with us in it. From two hundred years ago and more — it's hard to believe, but . . ." He glanced up at the chink, dark now except for the light of a single cold but steady star. "We've got to dig out more than ever now," he said, "and soon — tomorrow, or whenever he goes out next. And we've got to take the circlet — the plate, I mean — with us. I just pray it's not too late. Well, you heard him," he said as Melissa looked at him quizzically. "It sounds as if he wants to starve the whole village out and force us to help him do it, to make up for — for what happened centuries ago." He put his hands on her shoulders, gripping them painfully, his eyes probing hers. "Melissa, come on! You don't want to be a priestess, do you, a priestess of the Old Ways, whatever they are — *his* priestess?"

Melissa shook her head, his words barely penetrating, and pulled away. All she could think of, despite her own arguments to herself, was the last part of the diary, and that no one knew how the first Eli Dunn had died, or even if he had, or much of anything else that had happened in 1725. "Jed," she whispered, glancing toward the fire where the hermit sat, still as an ancient monument, staring into the flames, "Jed, who *is* he?"

But for that, Jed had no answer.

"I want every man you have, Chief, first thing in the morning. Every man you can spare, anyway."

"But, Mr. Dunn, begging our pardon, sir, we've already searched. We scoured the woods right after the children turned up missing. We put an all-points out all over the northeast and up into Canada — descriptions, everything. And the hermit's on every wanted list in the country by now. I'm sorry, I know how you must feel, but we've really done everything that can be done."

"You've given up, *that's* what you've done."

"If you'd only come earlier, sir," said the chief tiredly, "begging your pardon again, you could have helped with the search. But now . . ."

Stanley Dunn put his two hands on the chief's desk and leaned closer. "Look here," he began.

But then both men jumped, startled, for the door of the police station burst open, admitting a small redheaded boy in a green acorn cap, a sleek golden dog, and a tall, somewhat scruffy-looking man in wrinkled clothes.

"Oh, good grief," said Chief Dupres, covering his face with his hands.

200

"See," Tommy panted, tugging at Seth's sleeve. "What did I tell you? It's him, I know it is! Come on — you've got to go now!"

Suddenly Dunn looked from the boy to the man to the dog, and back to the man again, mystified. But then Seth took a step forward, holding out his hand. "I'm Seth Ellison," he said gravely. "The boy's father. This here's Tommy Coffin, in your girl's class, and this — well, this is sort of my son's dog . . ."

"Ulfin," put in Tommy eagerly. "His name's Ulfin." The dog's tail wagged as soon as his name was spoken.

"Ulfin," repeated Seth. "You want to take another look for the kids soon's it's light tomorrow, why, I guess we're game. Long's the chief here gives permission . . ."

Chief Dupres let his hands fall away from his face. "They say a little trickle of water," he remarked wearily, looking at Tommy, "can wear away a boulder if it drips on it long enough. And, by jingo, to get you here, Seth . . . ! Well, go ahead, then — I'd want to myself, if it was my kids. Just — well, for Pete's sake, be careful, and don't go mucking about with the evidence if you go out to the hermit's. Not that we've found much of anything. But still, don't move things around . . ."

Stanley Dunn's face broke into a huge grin and he pumped Chief Dupres's hand up and down. "Thanks, Chief," he said, "I knew you'd come around." Then he flung one arm across Seth's shoulders and the other over Tommy's. "Come on," he said, "I'll buy you a beer, Ellison — how about a Coke or something, Tom? We've got a lot of talking to do."

201

"Coffee," said Seth firmly when Tommy shot him a look. "I'm — er — on the wagon. Trying to be, anyway."

"Coffee it is," said Mr. Dunn, leading the two of them and Ulfin, who was shaking his head in annoyance at the muzzle, across the green to his car. "We'll go up to my mother's, then; she makes the best coffee in the state of New Hampshire. Maybe even the whole world . . ."

18

Melissa tossed restlessly on her rag bed, trying to sleep. A glimmer of light showed through the chink above her head — moonlight or dawn, she couldn't tell. But it's probably the last time, she told herself, trying to believe that it was: I'll be in my bed at Gran's the next time I sleep.

They had planned it carefully, in whispers, pretending to sleep while the hermit continued to sit by the fire as if in a trance. As soon as he left them to get wood — for that would take longer than getting water and they would need more before another day passed — as soon as he left, they would climb up to the chink and pry at the small stones around it till they fell away, opening their route to freedom. And then, Melissa thought, trying to snuggle down in her rag bed — but it was impossible — and then all we'll have to do is take the plate and run through the forest, safely home to Gran's . . .

Sleepily now, she pictured it: the kitchen fireplace, Pride and Joy on the hearth, Gran comfortably stirring one of her wonderful stews, smiling, opening her arms wide to welcome them home . . .

But Gran faded and her kitchen turned into the Boston one a few days after Mum's death, when Daddy had come in, tears suddenly on his cheeks when he caught Melissa trying to remember how her mother had made his favorite lentil soup . . .

And the kitchen gave way to Melissa's old bedroom — though Melissa twisted and turned on her rag bed trying to drive the memory away. But it kept coming back clearly: the night her mother died, Daddy sitting on the edge of Melissa's bed, rubbing her back and saying through his tears, "Pigeon, Pigeon, please say something — cry, scream, anything!"

What did he think, she wondered suddenly, when she hadn't been able to cry?

"Daddy — Daddy," Melissa heard herself say softly. "Daddy, I'm . . ."

Sorry, she'd been going to say: *Daddy, I'm sorry.*

But — it was best not to think about Daddy. He was far away anyway. It was best not to dwell on thoughts of him.

Melissa turned over, squirming to dig a Melissa-shape in the rags. But it was impossible to find a comfortable spot; she wondered if it was any easier for Jed, with his spare boy's body.

At last she slept fitfully, hovering around the edges of her familiar dream, with new fragments added:

the hermit in his white robe with the gold belt trying to bring her mother back from the dead with one of his obscure ceremonies; herself as Tabitha, not Melissa, married to Jed-Eben, but somehow still her own age, living back in 1725 in Fours Crossing — then herself as Priestess of the Temple of Spring, locked up forever in the hermit's cave tending the True Circlet in the wall above the altar, seeing people only once a year at Spring Festival, doomed to live as a sort of Vestal Virgin, forever . . .

Straight and true as the surest bloodhound, Ulfin led the two men and Tommy through the woods to the hermit's house, not even pausing to sniff the spot, now buried under new snow, where he had lain hurt and aching after the hermit had hit him and captured the Children.

"He's sure got no doubt," panted Seth Ellison as they approached the clearing. "Lord, he's a strong one!" — for Ulfin, leashed as well as muzzled, was pulling Seth nearly off his feet.

"What did I tell you?" Tommy cried triumphantly as Ulfin, his nose tight against the ground as if trying to catch a scent from deep under the snow, ran around one side of the house after a quick indifferent sniff at the front door. He pulled the leash so taut that Seth had to lean back with all his weight to hold him.

"Look at him!" cried Tommy, following. "He knows something — I bet he smells them!"

Ulfin whined, pawing the snow impatiently when Seth made him stop. Finally he barked, with his nose pointing toward the forest behind the house.

But Melissa's father was still at the front door, trying to force it open. "He did sniff here first," he called to Tommy and Seth. "I think we'd better have a look inside, just in case."

"But Ulfin wants to go on," Tommy insisted. "Maybe they were here and then left."

"No, Mr. Dunn's right, lad," said Seth, tugging Ulfin's leash again. "Come on, Ulfin, let's have a look. Come on, boy!"

Ulfin stood firm in the snow, his legs far apart, not moving except for the quivering of his nostrils.

The two men exchanged a doubtful glance over the top of Ulfin's head, but Tommy knelt down and took Ulfin's paw. "What is it, Ulf? Where are they?"

"Well," said Stanley Dunn impatiently, "I'm going to check the house. You want to stay with the dog, Tommy, okay — but you better tie him to a tree or something so he doesn't get away. Or better yet, bring him — he might smell something out. It won't take a minute as soon as we get this blasted door open."

Seth gave Tommy an apologetic glance, said, "Heel!" sharply to Ulfin, and went — pulling hard on the leash, for Ulfn knew nothing of heeling — to help with the door.

Melissa felt someone shaking her and opened her eyes to see Jed's face close to hers. "Good morning," he whispered. "It's as we hoped. There's almost no wood left — he'll have to go out today."

Melissa threw off her rag covers and jumped to her feet, glancing up at the chink. It seemed lighter outside — too bad, for it would have been safer to have fresh snow to cover their tracks as they escaped. But she was too elated at the prospect of leaving to really worry.

Jed put his finger to his lips — the hermit was up and muttering. Then he reached for Melissa's hand, and for a second their eyes locked, sharing their secret.

The hermit, grumbling, stirred the ashes in the firepit and blew on them, feeding the feeble glow with the few remaining sticks from the woodpile. He ladled the last of yesterday's water from the leather bucket into the kettle and threw in roots for their morning tea. Finally he spoke, scowling, apparently oblivious of the empty bucket and diminished woodpile. "It is too light outside," he growled, pointing to the chink. "We must perform the Ceremony before we break our fast. Quickly, Eben."

Impatiently, Jed went to the table, picking up the paper and reading the strange words:

> Eb dedne dloc sretniw
> Ew devas, gnirb srewolf . . .

The hermit hastened into his white robe while Jed chanted, and then he beckoned to Melissa to hand him the plate. "Stand near Eben," he snarled, grabbing the plate roughly from her. "If you must be made priestess, you may as well begin now. Say the words with him, and think of cold and darkness — for it lightens still, it lightens!"

Melissa went obediently to the table, though she felt as impatient as Jed still looked, and the hermit solemnly circled the smoking fire, carrying the plate.

"I wish he'd hurry up," Jed grumbled under his breath when Melissa leaned over the table to see the words.

"Again!" the hermit shouted urgently. "Begin again! All of us must now say it, lest it weaken further. Eb dedne . . ."

"Eb dedne dloc sretniw," intoned Melissa hesitantly, a half beat behind Jed so she could be sure of the pronunciation. It was strange how much like English the words sounded, even though of course they couldn't be English at all: "Ew devas, gnirb srewolf/Raeb gnivil ew . . ."

Strange, she thought, her voice continuing but her mind stuck at the second *ew*; what a funny word, and how funny we sound saying it: *ew*. It's almost as if we . . .

She blinked in surprise, hardly noticing that her voice had now stopped altogether.

Ew.

We.

Ew could be *we* backward, in one of the simplest of all ciphers — a simple, basic transposition cipher — the first kind she'd ever learned . . .

The hermit didn't seem to notice that Melissa had stopped chanting, but Jed glanced up at her, annoyed, till she shook her head and pointed first to the *w* and then the *e* in *ew* to show him what she'd learned.

But he was too busy chanting to notice, or at least to acknowledge what she'd found.

The hermit looked toward her, so she picked up

the chant again quickly — but *eb*, she realized, the other two-letter word, could be *be*, and *dloc* — yes, that was *cold* backward . . .

Once inside the hermit's house, Ulfin stopped resisting Seth's pull on his leash and ran immediately to the bare room. He flung himself at the nearly invisible door next to the fireplace and scratched frantically at it.

"But there's nothing here, lad." Seth frowned, examining what to him looked like a plain wall. "Nothing at all except a bit of a crack."

Stanley Dunn, who had gone into the other room first, came in and ran his hand along the wall the way his daughter had done, but unlike her, his hand missed the knot that opened the door. "Nothing here," he repeated after a minute. "Nothing but a wall. Still, old houses did sometimes have funny fireplace closets . . ."

"I hate to say it, Tom," said Seth, turning, "but — well, do you suppose maybe the poor old dog's gone crackers? Cooped up in that cage and all? You lose your smeller, old son?" he said to Ulfin. "Maybe," he said apologeticaly to Stanley, "it was just a rabbit or something he smelled out there behind the house. Sorry, old man. Lord." he sighed, closing his eyes, "I wish I had a drink!"

Tommy glanced apprehensively at Seth's back pocket, where he knew Seth sometimes carried a flask.

Seth saw and smiled ruefully. "Wishing's not having. Tom. I'll always wish, I guess, in a tight spot.

But I'll try not to have. That's the best I can do — okay?"

"Okay," Tommy said with relief, turning to the wall again; Ulfin was now sniffing along the place where floor and wall joined, whining. "There *must* be something here — a secret door or something. We just can't find it, is all. It must be hidden somehow. But there's got to be a way to open it!"

He pushed his way between the two men and felt the wall himself. As he did, Ulfin, as if unable to be patient a moment longer, jumped on him, throwing him off balance. Tommy thrust both his hands flat against the wall to break his fall.

And the door swung open without any of them noticing the knot that concealed the secret spring.

Before they could move or even speak, Ulfin darted inside the closet-like room, pulling Seth's arm out straight as he extended his leash to its fullest limit. "Ulfin!" Seth shouted — but by then Ulfin was back beside them again, depositing something at Stanley Dunn's feet, wagging his tail in triumph.

And then again before any of them could react, he leaped forward, snapping his leash out so sharply that he wrenched it out of Seth's hand. With one sharp bark, like a command, Ulfin pushed his way out the door and ran swiftly into the forest.

"It — it's a ribbon, a hair ribbon," Stanley Dunn said in an oddly choked voice, staring at the object Ulfin had dropped at his feet.

Tommy stared, too. "It's Melissa's," he said with great certainty. "She wore a green ribbon to school the day — the day she and Jed disappeared." Excitedly he ran to the door. "Come on!" he shouted impatiently to the two men. "Let's follow Ulfin before we lose him!"

"Come *on*, Melissa," Jed said impatiently, climbing up onto the stool, which he'd set on the table; the hermit had finally left with the empty bucket and a saw. "You can do that later; it's not really important anyway. Hand me that tray — Uh!" he grunted, stretching up toward the chink. "It's going to be harder than we thought — *Melissa!* Come on, hang on to the stool, will you? Or do you really want me to fall off and break my neck?"

"Sorry," Melissa said. She picked up the tray, and handed it to Jed. Then she took a firm grip on the stool, which wiggled precariously as Jed chopped at the stones around the chink. "Of course I don't want you to break your neck. But it *is* important, Jed; it's the Festival song. I think it is, anyway." She looked down at the words she'd scratched on the stone floor with a bit of charred stick from the firepit. "The words in the lines are backwards, I think, as well as the letters. And the words are different — more old-fashioned — but it's the same idea. Oh, come on," she said impatiently as Jed, banging away with the tray, only grunted at her discovery. "Listen — it'll just take a minute."

Without waiting for his answer, she read out what she'd scratched on the floor:

> Winter's cold ended be
> Flowers bring, saved we

211

> Living tree we living bear
> From true circlet, silver, rare . . .

That's as far as I got, but . . ."

The stool swayed dangerously, nearly sending Jed to the flood. *"Melissa!"* he said again, angrily this time.

"I know, I know," she said, "hold on to the stool; I'm sorry. It's just that — well, not only does it fit, but if we don't get out of here, Jed, we . . ."

"We'll get out," he said grimly.

She glanced up at him skeptically; she had already noticed that none of the stones had moved at all, despite his pounding.

"If we don't get out," she went on stubbornly, "I think maybe we can counteract the hermit's Ceremony and at least save the village . . ."

"Ha!" Jed snorted, turning around at last. "You mean you finally believe in it? Practical, scientific Melissa . . ."

"I don't know what I believe," she retorted angrily. "All I know is that if saying this thing backward makes it dark and snowy, maybe if it's said forward it'll work the other way around — Jed, why are you so mad?"

Jed was pounding furiously at a small rock. "Because," he gasped between blows, "we've finally — got — a chance to — get out of here and — all — you — can do is . . . Yikes! Melissa, look out!"

Just in time, Melissa ducked, narrowly escaping the small stone that plummeted to the floor.

"We're not," Jed shouted jubilantly, his anger suddenly gone, "going to have to say anything frontward *or* backward — not here, anyway — because — we're — going — to — get — out — oh, *blast* it, anyway, I've bent the stupid thing! Oh, rats! Double rats!"

"Maybe it'll be better for prying, though, now that it's bent," Melissa suggested.

But although Jed tried that, and went on banging as best he could with his inadequate tool, not another stone budged.

"Let me have a turn," said Melissa as Jed dropped his arm, exhausted and covered with perspiration despite the damp chill air of the cave.

He nodded dumbly, handed her the tray, and started to climb down.

But just as he was about to jump off the table, he froze, holding up one hand. "Hey," he whispered, "what's that? You hear it?"

"No," said Melissa, after straining for a moment to hear.

"It's stopped," he said, still whispering. "Wait — there it goes again."

This time Melissa did hear it, a muffled, scraping sound. "It's the hermit coming back," she said frantically. "Quick!" She tugged at Jed's hand. "Oh, quick, Jed, hurry!"

But he pulled away from her, still frowning. "No, wait — shh. It doesn't sound as if it's coming from there. And anyway, he never makes any noise. It sounds — it sounds," he said, standing up on the table, his face breaking into a joyful smile, "as if if it's right outside here. Melissa — it sounds like digging!"

Melissa climbed up on the table then, too, her

heart pounding and her breath coming fast — and then suddenly she knew he was right. It was a quick, sharp, scraping sound, not like a person digging, quite, but digging nonetheless. It was almost like . . .

Suddenly another small stone fell, and right after it, a third, a larger one this time — and then two pale-gold paws and a dusty, black, muzzled nose broke through the chink. Indignantly, Melissa jumped up, ripped the muzzle off, and unclipped the leash. A happy wet tongue licked her face, and for a moment she buried her hands in soft golden fur.

"You're alive!" she whispered. "Oh, wonderful, beautiful Ulfin, you're alive!"

"Quick," said Jed, "help him dig! Or take the stones — Look out, there's another one coming down. Oh, good dog, Ulfin, best of all possible dogs, good, good dog!"

"Aaaaaaaaiiiiiieeeeeeee!"

Jed whirled and Melissa tried to hide Ulfin, but the bitter, rasping cry was followed by angry words: "What is this? The traitor dog come again? You — Eben, Tabitha, Ulfin, all of you — betraying me once more. Aaaaaiiieeee!"

The hermit's hand, holding the plate as a weapon, lifted high above his head as Jed leaped down off the table to face him.

19

For the smallest part of a second there was no sound in the cave, and no motion. Then a lithe gold shape hurtled through the widened chink, sending down a shower of small stones, moss, and dirt. At the same time, from outside, distant but distinct, came an urgent, excited shout.

The hermit cried out again and drew back his arm to strike — but Ulfin streaked past Jed and Melissa, over their heads, and caught him squarely in the chest with the full force of his catapulting body. The plate flew out of the hermit's hand; Melissa reached out to try to catch it and missed, but she managed to deflect it toward Ulfin, who picked it deftly up in his teeth a second after it hit the ground. With a triumphant, almost saucy swing of his tail, he gathered his body for another leap.

The sound of voices outside grew louder. Melissa

was sure she heard a boy shout, "Over here!" — but by then Ulfin had jumped onto the table and was whining, tossing his head toward the chink — heavily, because of the weight of the plate — and pawing the tabletop impatiently.

"Quick!" Jed shouted — and though Melissa heard an ominous rustle behind them from where the hermit lay, she did not turn but instead helped Jed to boost Ulfin up to the chink and out.

"Run, good dog, run," Jed said under his breath. "Run as you've never run before . . ."

"Begone from the forest of winter!" the hermit shrieked then from behind them, rising unsteadily, lifting his gnarled arms, reeling toward them — but as they shrank back in terror, darkness filled the chink and a voice shouted "Melissa!" — and then Melissa was no longer aware of anything except two strong arms lifting her up and out into crisp cold air and freshly falling snow. She clung to the firm, reassuring body and rubbed her face against the familiar roughness of a cheek she had not dared acknowledge till a few hours earlier she'd missed — and loved — quite so much. A big hand smoothed her filthy hair, and a voice she had feared she might never hear again said, "Pigeon, my Pigeon — oh, thank God!"

When she looked down into the cave again, with her father's arm safe around her, it was to see Jed and his father and Tommy staring in disbelief at the side wall at the other end of the cave.

"If I didn't know I hadn't touched a drop all day," Seth was saying, rubbing his chin, "I'd swear I was drunk."

Melissa realized the hermit was no longer in the cave, and she raised her eyebrows inquiringly at Jed; he nodded.

"It's the way we think he brought us in," Jed explained to his father — Melissa noticed both of them were smiling shyly but not quite looking at each other — but she saw Seth's hand move to Jed's shoulder, and stay there till Jed moved. "We never could figure out how he did it," Jed continued. "Some kind of secret spring, I think, but . . ."

"Like the one back at the house for that closet-thing," said Tommy. "We found your hair ribbon, Melissa — well Ulfin did . . ."

But then even Tommy fell silent, looking at the blank wall — or the nearly blank wall, for now Melissa saw that again there was a little damp snow along one section of it.

"Wait," said Tommy suddenly, reaching up to a candle sconce that was right next to the square stone slab Melissa had noticed earlier. "Look — there's a bit of cloth here — as if it caught there from someone's clothes. I bet . . ." He reached up and tried to turn the sconce.

For a moment, nothing happened, but then suddenly, as Tommy twisted and pressed and turned, the squarish rock slab swung briefly open so fast that none of them really saw it clearly, pivoting as if fastened to a pole running through its center. For less than a second it stood open, perpendicular to the cave's wall, like one section of a revolving door. And then, without really seeming to stop, it swung closed again, sweeping a thin line of snow inside.

"Wow," said Jed, looking up at Melissa. "*That* can't be left over from the Old Times."

"There must be another thing to push on outside," said Tommy. "Push and turn — that's what I had to do, like one of those childproof bottles."

"No wonder he did all that whirling whenever he went out," Melissa said, "to distract us."

Jed twisted the sconce, making the door open again, and unsuccessfully tried to stop it from closing.

"That old hermit sure must be quick," said Tommy. "He must've had to practice a lot to get in and out without being squashed."

Jed turned away. "Trouble is," he said as if to himself, "he's got to be out in the forest somewhere, maybe partway to Fours Crossing by now. And he must be pretty mad . . ."

"Police'll find him," Seth Ellison said gruffly, following Jed and standing awkwardly behind him. "They'll find him. No one could get very far in this snow, 'specially an old man like him. Snow's deep, after all — falling fast now, too."

"I bet Ulfin could find him," Tommy said loyally as the three of them still in the cave lined up to climb out.

"Darned awkward doorway," grumbled Seth, who was the first to struggle through the opening and jump down from the large rock that served as a step up to the chink, which itself was some distance off the ground. (Of course, Melissa thought; how else would the light from the true circlet hit the *top* of the pine tree?) "No wonder the old man had another way out," Seth said when he'd jumped down.

Tommy followed easily, being smaller, and then

Jed, who looked curiously back at the cave as soon as he was on the ground again. "You can't really tell it's here, can you?" he said. "Unless you're looking for it, it just looks like a big heap of rocks in the middle of a lot of pine trees."

"The snow helps hide it, too," said Melissa's father. "It's a good thing we had the dog." He looked at Seth Ellison. "Snow'll cover the old man's tracks . . ."

Seth went around to the other side of the cave. "There's nary a sign of that door on the other side either," he said, coming back, "except a sort of sticking-out rock. And piles of snow on each side, where he's kept it clear enough to use, or where the door's swept the snow away. There's no sign of tracks either."

Jed gave Melissa a significant glance, and though she was uncomfortable with the thought, she had to agree when he whispered, "This snow's no accident."

But then there was Ulfin again, tail wagging, leaping up and down on them, licking their faces like an exuberant puppy instead of the hero he was. Behind him were Chief Dupres and three of his men. "There you are," the chief called jovially. "Safe and sound, I see. And the missing plate's been returned, thanks to our friend here." He stooped and patted Ulfin. "Odd coincidence," he said, "the plate, I mean."

"The hermit had it," Jed said quietly.

The chief looked surprised. "But what . . ."

"The hermit," said Melissa's father grimly, "had the children. Holed up in this cave."

The chief's grin faded and he peered into the

chink when Stanley Dunn pointed it out to him. "So it's kidnapping, after all," he said soberly. "And probably burglary, too." He glanced quickly around the pine grove. "But where's the suspect? Did he hurt you kids?" he asked, looking at Melissa. She shook her head.

"Suspect, ha!" Seth snorted. "He did it, all right. And he ran off, of course."

"Pretty light-footed," said the chief, peering down at the trackless snow, "isn't he? A plague on this weather! Well," he said, though a little doubtfully, "we'll soon have him. If I might just borrow this wonderful dog, Jethro? I hear he's your . . ."

"Where's his muzzle?" Tommy asked Melissa in an undertone.

"I took it off." They exchanged a grin. "The chief doesn't seem to have noticed."

Jed was kneeling in the snow, hugging Ulfin. "Sure, you can borrow him," he said, and then he whispered into Ulfin's ear as if wishing him good luck.

The chief and his men went off, leading Ulfin.

And then Melissa, Jed, Tommy, and the two men tramped happily through the forest, home to Gran's.

It was as if the hugging, the explaining, the laughing, and the crying would never stop, and it seemed as if most of the village gathered at Gran's that afternoon to welcome them. A cheer went up as they approached — Melissa and her father trudging across the field with their arms around each other; Jed walking between Tommy and Seth, a hand shyly on each of their shoulders, Tommy's eyes never leaving Jed's face and Jed for once not seeming to mind; and then Gran — Gran on her snowshoes with the bindings loose, running across the field to meet them, laughing and crying all at once — and then running home ahead of them to somehow put together an enormous meal that it seemed all the village helped them to eat . . .

When the meal was over, there was a knock at the door and Ulfin burst in ahead of Chief Dupres, making Pride and Joy flee in terror to the mantelpiece, knocking over two candlesticks and a vase as he went. "Darn dog," said the chief affectionately, stomping snow off his boots. "Wouldn't let me rest till I'd brought him here. Far as I'm concerned, he can have anything he wants — he got our man, he did!"

Ulfin leaped on Jed, on Melissa, and on Tommy, licking their faces again and wagging his tail so hard that Gran, behind him, laughed and pretended to shiver in the breeze he stirred up.

Finally he settled down with his head in Jed's lap.

"Dad?" Jed asked, looking up at Seth, who had lifted his hand from Jed's shoulder only long enough to eat Gran's wonderful meal. "Do you think maybe we could keep him?"

"Just try to give him to anyone else," said Seth with a smile.

Jed smiled back — tentatively, as if he still couldn't believe the change in his father. As if he wasn't going to question it much either, at least not for now.

Tommy dug into his pocket and brought out a grimy, yellowish piece of paper. "License," he said gruffly, handing it to Jed. "See — your name's on it."

Jed looked at Tommy in astonishment. "You mean you . . . ?"

"Jed, you know what," said Seth, clearing his throat. "You — you've got quite a pal here. It's not just the license, although that, too. But — well, without Tom here, we'd never have found you and" — Seth waggled Tommy's cap — "and I'd still be sitting home in the old red chair."

Melissa saw Tommy blush again, especially when Jed reached across Seth for his hand. "Hey," he said, shaking it. "Hey, listen, any time you want to borrow a good dog . . ." Jed's face got a little red, too, but his eyes held Tommy's for a long, steady moment and then he said softly, "Thanks, Tom. You're okay."

Tommy buried his face so deep in Ulfin's fur his cap fell off. Jed scooped it up and, with an exaggerated sweeping gesture that made them both laugh, clapped it back onto his head . . .

". . . Are you sure there are no other charges we should — er — bring against the old man?" the chief was saying to Stanley Dunn and Gran near the door, where, Melissa realized, they'd been talking while she'd been watching Tommy and Jed. "You sure the children told you nothing else?"

Gran shook her head and went to the stove to pour the chief a cup of coffee. "No, nothing," she said. "They're both fine."

"Well," said the chief, taking the coffee, "thank you, Miz Dunn — that's a blessing." He shook his head. "We sure had a time with the old man. Charley's got him down at the station now, booking him. We'll hold him here in Fours Crossing overnight — too snowy to chance the roads in the dark — and we'll take him to Hiltonville in the morning." He looked around at all of them. "Just wanted to let you folks know, so's you could rest easy tonight. Must have been pretty darn scary," he said to Jed and Melissa, "if he acted as crazy with you kids as he did with us."

Jed glanced at Melissa and then said, with exaggerated casualness, "What do you mean? In what way crazy?"

"Well," said the chief, sipping his coffee, "he kept muttering, like — saying all these weird things — as if the weather'd driven him batty or maybe his run through the woods before we got him. When we finally caught up to him, he yelled like a — well, like a madman — all those curses he used to say at Festival time. It's okay then, of course — part of the show — but it just didn't make any sense when he did it today."

"Cold and endless winter?" Tommy asked eagerly. "And the icicles one — impaling your hearts — that one?"

"Yep," said the chief. He put down his cup and stood. "What got me, though," he said, shaking his head, "was what he said at the very end, just when Charley and the others were about to take him into the station. He'd been fighting us hard — it took all of us to hold him at first — but he stopped at the door and got real calm all of a sudden. Then he kind of looked around and across the green toward the

223

Ellison statue, and he kind of held up his hand like he was making a speech or something, and he said, real slow, 'I — will — return.' Just like that, over and over — and solemn, like he really thought he would. Gives me the creeps, just telling about it."

Jed froze at the words, his hand on Ulfin's head; Melissa felt her fingers gripping her father's; he looked down at her in surprise and said to the chief, as if to reassure her, "Well, but he won't return, though, will he, Chief? I mean, he'll be put away now, won't he?"

"I shouldn't wonder," said the chief. " 'Course there'll be a trial, and — well, I shouldn't speculate beforehand, but my guess is that he'll be sent to a mental home or to jail — one of the two, I should think, for sure. No, I don't think anyone's going to have to worry about him being out there in the woods for a good long while, if ever again."

Melissa shivered, wishing she could be sure that was true. And then thoughts that had been forming in her mind since the hermit had told them about the true Ceremony began to take firmer shape — thoughts about the Old Ways and the New, and how, from what Eben's diary had said as well as from what the hermit had told them, it seemed as if the people in Fours Crossing who had started the New Ways hadn't at first been sure enough of either the New Ways or of themselves to let the Old Ways continue, and that somehow that was part of what had driven the hermit mad, even centuries later. And maybe, she thought, the first Eli Dunn was driven mad by it, too — and maybe much later the people of the village were ashamed of that, and so removed the religion chapter from the history book and threw away the records for 1725.

She thought at first that it would be too complicated to say all that, except perhaps later to Jed, but much to her own surprise as well as everyone else's, she did end up saying some of it, as much as she could without having to go into too many complicated background explanations. "It's kind of sad," she finished, "if the hermit *is* crazy. Of course he's — well, awful — and I was terrified of him. But all the same, it's as if it maybe isn't all his fault — how he is, I mean. It's as if he let himself get all — twisted inside because — because he couldn't accept the truth."

"Shh, Pigeon, honey, take it easy," said her father, stroking her hair. "It's all right now, it's all over."

But Gran looked steadily at her, as if she understood. "What is the truth, Melissa?" she asked softly.

"That things change," Melissa answered slowly. "That nothing — nothing stays the same. People die. They change inside themselves, too, and they change how they think. You can keep bits of old things — the way Fours Crossing kept bits of the Festival . . ."

"The song," Jed said, as if privately to her. "You're right! The old words were different, but — as you said — still the same."

Melissa nodded. "It's all mixed up," she said, rubbing her forehead as if it ached — which it did, a little. "Things change, but it's hard to accept it. I know how — how the hermit must have felt. I think I do, anyway. He was so *sad* underneath. But —

well, each way is right for its own time, I guess. Things have to grow" — she looked up at her father — "no matter what."

Gran reached out to Melissa and gently touched her face. "You're your mother's daughter," she said, so no one but Melissa and her father could hear. "She'd have seen what you've seen, lambie, understood what you understood. So part of her goes on living through you."

Melissa's eyes were wet but clear. She nodded at Gran, and saw her father nod also.

"Good," Gran said, smiling at both of them. "Now, Chief," she said, getting up and taking his empty cup, "suppose tomorrow morning . . ."

It was then that Jed caught Melissa's eye and dipped his head toward the dining room.

Melissa had known, of course, that this moment would come. Faith, she said to herself now; faith as well as change; faith even when you don't understand.

The thought steadied her as she followed Jed into the dining room and closed the door.

They stood for a long moment facing the four softly gleaming silver plates, back at last in their original positions.

"What do you think?" asked Jed.

Melissa turned to the window. A blustery north wind was howling outside, pushing itself under the eaves and rattling the shutters.

"I think," she said quietly, "that we still have one more thing to do."

*　　　*　　　*

And so on Saturday morning, as the weak sun glowed palely in the gray and dismal sky, Jed, Tommy, and Melissa, with Ulfin trotting beside them, carefully carried the little pine tree, some of its needles now beginning to turn yellowy-brown, from Gran's hill down to the village. No one else would help except Susie. Spring Festival had already been held, everyone said as kindly as they could; no one had the heart to repeat it. Better just go on with the town's business, especially after everything that had happened. Spring would come in its own time, probably — there was no point in getting the youngest children all excited again for nothing. And so on.

It was a forlorn little procession that made its way silently down Gran's hill to the village and lifted the tree to the sleigh which Mr. Coffin had reluctantly left standing outside the Post Office for them. They had no idea, of course, if it would work — if the equinoctial light that had given spring to the tree on Spring Festival in a modified, newer ceremony would have any power now — or if indeed it had ever really had any. But they knew they had to try.

"All right, Susie," said Jed. Tommy led his little cousin to the front of the sleigh, where Melissa stood waiting. It didn't seem to matter to Susie that the procession was so small.

"The tree looks sort of happy," Tommy whispered to Melissa, straightening his green cap as they took their places. "I don't know — it looked terrible when we took it down the hill, but it looks better now."

Melissa looked up and was surprised to see that Tommy was right. It did look better — greener, somehow, and its branches seemed almost bouncy again.

"You have the flowers?" Jed called down to her from the sleigh.

"Yes."

"I've got some, too," said Tommy.

"Good man, Tom," Jed said, and Tommy beamed.

The horse pawed the snow restlessly.

"All right, folks," called Jed, just as Selectman Ellison had done two months earlier. "Ready?"

"Yes," Tommy and Melissa called back.

The tiny procession moved forward, Ulfin in Mr. Henry Ellison's place, his proud golden head held high.

And then, very quietly Mr. Coffin came out of the Post Office, and Mr. Titus came out of the general store, and Mr. Ellison came out of the Selectmen's office, and Joan and Tim and Miss Laurent and some other people came out of their houses around the green. By the time the tiny procession had wound its slow way up to where the fourth silver plate shone clear and bright and brave through Gran's sparkling window, it wasn't so tiny any more. To be sure, it was only a handful compared to what it would have been had the whole village been there — but by the time it reached the top of the hill and was joined by a smiling Gran and by Seth Ellison and Stanley Dunn, there were enough people to separate in two halves to form the V, and more than enough people to fill the air with singing.

> Now the cold has gone away,
> Deck our tree with flowers gay.

This the tree the year has spared,
This the year that we have shared.

Forest spirit, hear our prayer:
  Bring the springtime!
  Bring the sunshine! . . .

"Look," said Melissa to her father, who had come to stand next to her. The clouds had broken and there was a bright patch of blue above their heads. He nodded and squeezed her hand.

As the snow melts, as the ice melts,
As the birds come, singing, to us,
Snowdrop, crocus, tulip for us . . .

On they sang, joyfully and with conviction, Melissa sometimes thinking of the old words as she sang the new. At the very end, they heard what sounded like an echo from the village. Melissa turned and looked down the hill and saw that the people left in the village were singing, too, and that the echo had been their voices, a beat or two behind those at Gran's.

Jed started to jump down from the sleigh to lift Susie up, but his father motioned to him to stay put and lifted her up himself. Solemnly, the little girl fastened a snowdrop to the tree — Gran's snowdrop, this time; her forced ones had luckily been late — as if, Melissa thought, they'd been waiting for this second Festival day.

The *V* straightened, and the procession marched down the hill to the village. Melissa felt her father reach for her hand again. "I walked like this with your mother," he whispered, "when we were first married. She looked as happy as you."

Tears — real, true tears — stung Melissa's eyes again, and she didn't try to keep them from spilling over. She looked up at her father and saw that his eyes were bright with tears, too. And she didn't mind.

Stanley Dunn took his hand away to put his arm around Melissa's shoulders, pulling her close. "You've been very brave, my pigeon," he said. "And I love you very much."

Melissa knew she was smiling even though the tears were running down her face now, and she knew she didn't care who saw, and she knew she'd never felt so absurdly happy or so sweetly sad all at the same time in her life before.

"She'd have liked this," Melissa said to her father after a while. She hesitated, then went on shyly. "Mumma would have liked it so much. I — I remember when we used to find the first crocus in Mrs. Halliday's yard on the Hill."

Daddy nodded and squeezed her shoulders. "I remember, too, Pigeon. You were both always so excited when you found it. Mumma loved springtime. We'll always remember that, won't we, and think of her in the spring?"

Emphatically, Melissa nodded, and her heart sang with her voice as the procession wound around the village. They sang at each house, picking up more and more people as they went, till by the time Susie and Ulfin led them slowly back up the hill, the whole village was there after all. Jed jumped down from the sleigh when the *V* formed outside Gran's again, and his father came to stand next to him with Melissa and her father and Gran. The words of the old song rose on the air for the last time that year as the gaily decked tree, the dog Ulfin proudly on guard beside it, was lifted down from the sleigh and placed outside Gran's window facing all the plates, but the fourth one most of all.

The sun felt warm on Melissa's back and made the daffodil at the tree's top glow as gold as Ulfin's collar.

And that night, the thaw began, and spring came at last to Fours Crossing.

Author's Note

"But," someone is sure to say, "there *isn't* any Fours Crossing, New Hampshire. There probably wasn't even any place like it way up north in the 1670s. No one's proved that root cellars were ever anything but root cellars. And people don't march around New England town greens carrying pine trees on the first day of spring."

True — and not true. Certainly there are many New England towns like Fours Crossing, even though there is no Fours Crossing. There *could* have been settlements in northern New Hampshire in the 1670s, and root cellars *could* have been other than root cellars. Perhaps people don't march around town greens on the first day of spring — but there are maypoles, and harvest festivals, and other seasonal celebrations with pagan origins. This book is based on things that *could* have happened, not on things that *did* happen.

But who knows?

Nancy Garden
Carlisle, Massachusetts

About the Author

Nancy Garden is a graduate of Columbia Teachers College. She has worked as an editor for an education magazine, a textbook publisher and as a literary agent. In addition, she has had jobs as a theatrieal lighting designer, actress, and stage manager. She has also written many books. Before moving to Carlisle, Massachusetts, she used to live in Brooklyn, New York.